A Cat of a Different Color

STEVEN BAUER

ILLUSTRATED BY TIM RAGLIN

DELACORTE PRESS

Published by
Delacorte Press
an imprint of
Random House Children's Books
a division of Random House, Inc.
1540 Broadway
New York, New York 10036

Visit us on the Web! www.randomhouse.com/kids
Educators and librarians, for a variety of teaching tools, visit us at
www.randomhouse.com/teachers

Library of Congress Cataloging-in-Publication Data

Bauer, Steven.
    A cat of a different color / Steven Bauer ; illustrated by Tim Raglin.
        p.   cm.
    Summary: An orphan girl and a strange cat save the villagers of Felicity-
by-the-Lake from the proclamations of a greedy, selfish and mean mayor.
    ISBN 0-385-32710-2
    [1. Orphans—Fiction. 2. Cats—Fiction. 3. Mayors—Fiction.] I. Raglin,
Tim, ill. II. Title.
PZ7.B32625 Cat 2000
[Fic]—dc21
                                                                99-047787

The text of this book is set in 12.5-point Meridien.
Book design by Debora Smith
Manufactured in the United States of America
June 2000

10 9 8 7 6 5 4 3 2 1

BVG

For Barbara and Charles Minor

Contents

CHAPTER

1

Felicity-by-the-Lake

In a village near a silver lake, at the bottom of a range of jagged mountains, three kittens were born in the same litter. Two of them were common enough. They had wide, astonished, watery blue eyes, and gray coats stippled with black, and paws as white as if they'd been dipped in heavy cream, and when the kittens were ten weeks old, those villagers who wanted a pet came round to the house where the kittens had been born and these two were quickly chosen.

Their names were Flumadiddle and Gigamaree, and until they grew to be a year old, they looked so very much alike that sometimes Mr. Mayapple, the man who chose poor Gigamaree, would call, "There you are, you worthless welp!" when he saw Flumadiddle. And sometimes Miss Gagney, who fussed and fiddled over Flumadiddle, would mournfully call, "Why do you disobey me? I saw you prowling outside last night!" This would sorely hurt Flumadiddle's feelings, for it was her brother Gigamaree who stalked the streets, while Flumadiddle was a close-to-the-fireside cat, and she knew it was Gigamaree whom Miss Gagney had seen.

But from the start no one mistook the third cat for anyone but himself. He had fur that seemed to shift in hue in the slightest breeze—fur the color of burning leaves, then fur the color of smoke. His eyes were the palest amber, and the hair on his belly was as whorled as the shapes the villagers' breath made on winter mornings. When he was still a tiny kitten, he'd fallen from a footstool into a large bucket of water, and rather than panicking, he'd seemed quite content to be soaked clear through—which was *very* odd, for most cats hate even the thought of getting wet. The villagers called him *the-cat-who-loves-water*, or, in the dialect of that part of the country, Ulwazzer, and because he was so strange, so unlike any cat that anyone had ever seen before, no one would take him home. He was preternaturally calm, they said, and probably possessed, and who wanted a cat who might raise the hair on your neck by yowling in the dark, who might turn on you when least expected, or leap on your face in the night?

For a while after Ulwazzer's brother and sister had been taken away, he was very lonely. As kittens the three had tumbled together, play-fighting, pouncing on bits of string, darting off with no warning as if the world were on fire. Now that the others had homes of their own, he rarely saw them, and when it became clear that both his parents and his parents' owners were wary of him, he understood that he would be forced to make his way in life by himself.

At first he roamed only as far as the lake outside of town. But as time passed he ventured farther and farther from home, until the wide world itself seemed the place he belonged. Still, sooner or later he always returned to the village where he'd been born, because it was the first place he'd seen when his eyes had opened, and because it was beautiful.

Now, this village was named Felicity-by-the-Lake, and the people who lived there were a contented and friendly bunch who liked each other and themselves and felt it was their good fortune to have found such a lovely and peaceable home. The village was small enough to be comfortable yet big enough to provide everything its inhabitants might need. Its streets were paved with cobblestones and lit at night by three-globed streetlamps. At its center stood a fountain and a statue of the town's first mayor, and all around the square were cafés and shops selling leather goods and lake-water taffy, silver tankards, and roasted meats on sticks.

In winter, when snow swirled down from the mountains and landed like thick icing on the thatched roofs of the village, people scurried through the streets with reddened cheeks, their hands tucked neatly into woolen muffs. The smell of woodsmoke and roasted chestnuts hung in the air, and down at the lake, skaters would glide over the ice in long glancing strides, scarves snug around their necks as they gazed upon the world's cold beauty.

In summer, the shores of the lake were dotted with picnic blankets, and the calm surface of the water was cut by swimmers and divers and splashers and boaters, all having a glorious time. After supper, as the sun began to drop behind the

range of jagged mountains, children would pour from their houses to play in the streets and surrounding fields. In the lingering twilight, when everything seemed bathed in liquid gold, their parents would sit on their porches and invite their neighbors over. Or they would dig deep in their pockets for their final hard-earned doon, which was the name of the money in Felicity-by-the-Lake, and walk to the square, where they would linger by the ice cream shop, or converse at the tables in front of the town's two cafés, or perhaps spend an hour at the cider parlor with its round concrete tables and accordion band. As they strolled down the street, they would pause when they met someone they knew (everyone in the village knew almost everyone else), and their quiet words and laughter would float on the breeze like music. Often the streets were filled until quite late, long after the three-globed streetlamps had been lit and the moon had risen from the east and drifted like a swan across the dark lake of the sky.

Felicity-by-the-Lake was a fine place to be a cat or dog as well, for almost everyone in the village had one or the other or several of both, and there were no leash laws and no barking regulations and few fences, and cats and dogs got along, on the whole, better here than they did anywhere else in the world.

Yet true to the sad fact that sometimes people who grow up in the same family drift apart, the cats named Flumadiddle and Gigamaree now had very little to do with their strange-looking brother Ulwazzer. They saw him from time to time, coming or going, but he was away a great deal, and they couldn't help feeling that there must be something wrong with him because *they* had been chosen and *he* had not.

They were older, if not wiser, now, and they had assumed their adult coats. For better or worse, everyone could distinguish them at a glance and never mistook them for one another. Gigamaree, who still lived with the bad-tempered Mr. Mayapple, was skittish and his gray fur was matted. He had a crooked tail from a door Mr. Mayapple had slammed in anger, and his disposition had turned quite mean. And Flumadiddle was still utterly spoiled by Miss Gagney. She had lost her kitten fur completely and had become a very large canvas of black, white, and brown splotches, with tufted ears and a grating *meeeow*. She was altogether lazy and vain and disdainful and very plump.

But the cat with fur the color of burning leaves

and fur the color of smoke still looked as he had when he'd been born. He lived where he would and came and went as he wished. He was unfettered, and he was at ease in the world, even though he very much would have liked a home of his own, a safe warm place to return to when life bore down too hard. Because they remained afraid of him, the villagers still wouldn't let him in their houses. But most every evening someone's good nature would rise like cream to the surface, and one or another would put out a little food for the strange wild cat who belonged to no one.

Mayor Hoytie and His Proclamations

Five years passed, and as happened every year at the end of January, it was time for the village to elect a new mayor. In a usual year, there were forums at the town hall, where candidates shook the grown-ups' hands and patted children on the head; there were droning speeches about Felicity-by-the-Lake, its history and future and its bright shining promise. One candidate would promote the rethatching of roofs, while the other would suggest new etched globes for the streetlamps. Rarely was there a fresh idea mentioned or a new plan proposed, but since Felicity-by-the-Lake was a prosperous and generally complacent little village, fresh ideas and new plans were not of much interest to the inhabitants.

But this winter had been an especially harsh winter, and the streets were thick with ice; most every day new snow fell, and the wind that howled down from the jagged mountains was cold enough to take your breath away. From the eaves of the houses, icicles sharp as daggers hung, and most people were more concerned with staying safe and warm than with electing a mayor. The villagers kept close to their hearths, and bundled their blankets more tightly around them, and the forums at the town hall were canceled.

This was unfortunate, because for the first time in recorded memory, one of the candidates had new ideas. He was Lyman Wilford, who, together with his wife, Betsy, ran the print shop. Lyman Wilford was honest and kind and serious-minded. His hands were always stained with printer's ink, and his clothes were smudged, and he wore a leather printer's apron wherever he went, even under his heavy winter coat. As he slipped and slid from door to door, he handed out leaflets he'd printed, which explained the sorts of things he wanted to do as mayor: build a new school (since the old one was now too small), and change the makeup of the village council, and buy new swings for the playground, for example.

The second candidate was Jeremiah Hoytie, who owned the newly established specialty shop where pâté and soft herbed cheeses and fresh-baked breads and cakes and roasted meats were sold at quite ridiculous prices. Everywhere he went, he walked mincingly in his hobnailed boots. He wore a high beaver hat and a long muskrat coat, and when he was invited inside (for no one wanted to stand at the door with the wind swooping in like a bandit to steal the warmth), he took off the coat to reveal a blue waistcoat studded with brass buttons that bristled whenever he took a breath. He was all broad smiles and bright hellos, all everything's-fine-and-couldn't-be-better, and he flattered the townspeople by telling them that Felicity-by-the-Lake was the very model of the modern en-lightened village and that not a thing needed changing. And as he went he handed out vouchers good at his shop for free hot chocolate and hand-dipped bonbons.

Though everyone liked Lyman Wilford—had known him for years and his parents before him—and though everyone liked his wife, Betsy, and their daughter, Anne, they thought perhaps he should have scrubbed his hands, removed his ink-splotched apron, and been a bit more sensitive to their feelings about the state of things in Felicity-by-the-Lake, especially during such a harsh winter. They did not want to pay more taxes to build a new school, and they thought the playground's swings were just fine. And even though Jeremiah Hoytie was new in town this past year and the villagers didn't really know anything about him, they admired his waistcoat with all the brass buttons, which seemed in a way like a mayor's coat, and they liked his smiles and his reassurances and his free hot chocolate. Perhaps most of all, they had quickly developed a liking for hand-dipped bonbons, and during the last week of January, Mr. Hoytie oversaw the creation of more of these sumptuous confections than can reasonably be believed.

So when election day arrived, blustery but clear, the villagers came forth from their houses to vote, and when the ballots were counted, the new mayor was found to be Jeremiah Hoytie.

Now, Hoytie was bespectacled and watermelon-bellied; he was fond of food and liked to stuff himself at all hours of the day, and he disliked exercise of any kind, with the sole exception of an occasional nightly stroll in the late spring and early fall of the year. On these strolls, which he undertook in total solitude, he considered subjects he thought profound: why gold was the world's most beautiful color, next to silver, and how owning things made people better than animals. His face above his coal-black beard was red as a sockeye salmon fillet, and though the villagers didn't yet know it, he was greedy and selfish and very mean.

Prucilla Hoytie, his wife, complained bitterly of fainting spells and general weakness, but in reality she was strong as a water buffalo. She was neither smart nor beautiful, clever neither with singing nor with drawing; she could not run very fast nor spell very well, though she considered herself exceptionally skilled at everything. In short, she had a very high opinion of herself for someone so ordinary. Her sole talent, it seemed, was an unfortunate gift for rhyming. Her pale fingernails were always frosted with silver and her yellow hair hung in ringlets on either side of her painted face. Her nose was long and thin, and so sharp it was rumored in the village that if she couldn't find a knife, she would sometimes use her nose to slice a cheese. Like her husband, she believed she had a profound side, which she indulged while lying in a rowboat on the lake, with someone else straining at the oars.

With Mr. and Mrs. Hoytie, in a large stone house on the edge of the village, lived two others: a young orphaned cousin named Daria, and the Hoyties' son, Sam. Mrs. Hoytie had suffered through a difficult delivery twenty-seven years before, due to Sam's exceptional size; he had been so large that the doctor who attended her had believed that Mrs. Hoytie would give birth to triplets. By now Sam had grown to be a large man, a *very* large man—a square-jawed, dim-witted, sad-eyed, thick-tongued, sausage-fingered giant of a man who always did what his mother and father told him.

When, late one night, under threat of the stocks or worse, the Hoyties had had to flee the last village where they'd lived, Sam had helped his mother and father load all their many belongings into a large wooden cart. Piled high with or-molu clocks and mahogany wardrobes, with feather-stuffed armchairs and sofas, with boxes of cutlery and crates of china, the cart had been very heavy indeed. But the horses were locked in the barn and there was no time to spare, so Sam just picked up the yoke and pulled—because his parents told him to.

* * *

As you have heard, Mr. Hoytie was greedy, selfish, and mean. In the town the Hoyties had lived in before, he had been the tax collector and had established cunning methods to enrich himself. And Mr. Hoytie had decided to run for mayor of Felicity-by-the-Lake not so much because he wished to be of service, but because he thought he would enjoy the prestige and because he and his wife had concocted new and inventive ways to make themselves richer and happier. They planned and they plotted as January turned to February and then to March, as the days grew longer and the sun moved higher in the skies, as the snow turned to rain and the icicles disappeared and the ground turned muddy.

On the first day of April, when spring had just arrived, Mayor Jeremiah Hoytie issued a proclamation:

All must be in their houses by dark!

This would allow the mayor to walk alone at night when he took his moonlit strolls, without fear of interruption. He went to his rival Lyman Wilford and ordered the man to print up, in great black letters on heavy paper, one hundred copies of the proclamation.

"Wait just a minute, Jeremiah," Lyman Wilford said. "Folks have been cooped up all winter long, and they'll want to stay out at night, now that the weather's improved. You can't go around making absurd laws. The people of this village won't stand for it."

"Why, indeed I can, and I shall," said Jeremiah Hoytie, sputtering.

"And what, if you don't mind my asking, is the reason behind this proclamation?"

"Reason?" asked Jeremiah Hoytie. "I'm the mayor! Do I need a better reason?"

"Yes," said Lyman Wilford. "I would imagine you do."

"Well then," Jeremiah Hoytie said, thinking quickly, "Why, because . . . uh . . . well, because . . ." *Now, why would people stay in after dark?* he wondered. Then it came to him. "Because there are wolves in the mountains who come down to the lake in the glimmering dark, and I, who am mayor, am responsible for the welfare of our children and their parents, and I want no one eaten by these lean and hungry wolves."

"Wolves in the mountains?" Lyman Wilford said. "First I've heard of it."

"Yes, wolves," said Jeremiah Hoytie, baring his

teeth and snarling. "Gray, nasty beasts with pointed snouts and sharp, white fangs and golden, gleaming eyes." And he turned his back and stalked triumphantly out of the printer's shop, sending Sam later that afternoon to fetch the posters and to plaster them on every kiosk and bulletin board and empty wall in town.

Lyman Wilford had been right; the townsfolk did not take kindly to this proclamation, and they complained bitterly. But at least, they thought, they still had plenty of daylight for boating and swimming in the lake.

One week later, when the grumbling in Felicity-by-the-Lake had simmered down, Mayor Jeremiah Hoytie issued Proclamation the Second:

At all times stay away from the lake!

He had always wanted to own a good-sized body of water, and this was surely his opportunity. Besides, he knew the nutritional value of fresh food, and now his son could shoot waterfowl and troll for fish undisturbed. The mayor went again to the printer's shop and ordered one hundred copies of the new proclamation.

"Hold it right there, Hoytie," Wilford said. "You can't do that. The people of this town have been swimming in that lake for as long as there's *been* a town, which is called, may I remind you, Felicity-by-the-*Lake*."

"I know very well the name of this town, of which, may I remind *you*, I am the mayor. Why, indeed I *can* keep people away from the lake, and I shall," said Jeremiah Hoytie, who this time had figured out a reason in advance. "I have recently discovered snapping turtles in the lake who might mistake a toe for a duckling, and I, who am mayor, am responsible for the welfare of our children and their parents, and I want no one chomped to pieces by these wild and savage turtles."

Lyman Wilford rolled his eyes. "But there have *never* been snapping turtles in the lake," he said.

"Well, there are now," said Jeremiah Hoytie, clacking his teeth together. "Horrid old things, with shells as big as a wagon wheel!" And he turned his back and stalked haughtily out of the printer's shop, sending Sam later that day to fetch the posters and to plaster them on every kiosk and bulletin board and empty wall in town.

This time the villagers' grumbling grew into shouts, and the people decided they would rather take their chances with the great wild outdoors than be sequestered after dark and forbidden to visit the lake, and so they swarmed through the streets in protest and massed before the mayor's house, waving their hands and yelling. They yelled for quite a long while, and at last Jeremiah Hoytie's face appeared at an upstairs window and some time later he flung open the front door and stood there in his blue waistcoat studded with brass buttons, but without holding a tray of bonbons.

"Go away!" he bellowed. Then he slammed the door, and no matter how much the people banged and yelled, he would not open it again.

The very next day the mayor issued Proclamation the Third:

No criticizing the mayor!
The breaking of any proclamation
will result in serious Fines!

This would have been merely silly were it not for the Hoyties' son, Sam, who, you will recall, was twenty-seven years old and a large man, a *very* large man—a square-jawed, dim-witted, sad-eyed, thick-tongued, sausage-fingered giant of a man. In the wake of the protest, the mayor appointed Sam the Village Constable. On the very afternoon that the third proclamation was plastered on every kiosk and bulletin board and blank wall in town, Sam began to make his rounds.

Whenever the villagers looked out their windows, they saw Sam skulking by, all seven feet of him, all two hundred and eighty-seven pounds of him, with his big rocklike jaw and his beetle brows and his close-set, quite small eyes. He prowled the village streets after dark; he kept an eye on the lake; he listened, whenever he could, to what people said. And if anybody disobeyed his father's rules, Sam lifted the offender by the ankles and carried him upside down all the way across town to his father's house and into his father's counting room, where the offender was fined three doons for each infraction, and his name was entered in a leather-bound ledger before he was released, and he was given until noon the next day to pay up.

Of course it wasn't only the *people* of Felicity-by-the-Lake who suffered as a result of Mayor Hoytie's edicts. Cats like Gigamaree loved to prowl the streets after dark, looking for a bit of excitement and perhaps a mouse or vole; and most dogs, of course, liked nothing better than a good swim and the chance afterward to run up to a total stranger and shake all over. As for criticizing the mayor—well, in the days following the posting of the third proclamation, Sam would often pass right by a huddle of cats or a riffraff of dogs and not understand a thing. But they kept their lawbreaking to that, for if they were caught after dark or by the lake, their people would have to pay the fine, and they didn't wish to bite the hands that fed them.

Oh, the mayor and his wife were greedy and selfish and mean, the villagers agreed, and they hated being kept in their houses and away from the lake. But if truth be told, they hated being held upside down by the ankles even more. They couldn't for the life of them imagine how they had elected Jeremiah Hoytie as their mayor when they'd had the choice of Lyman Wilford. But then they remembered the sweet and lingering taste of the hot chocolate and the hand-dipped bonbons and sighed. Oh, well, they said to one another; he would only be mayor until the end of the year.

And thus in the annoying way people have of being able to get used to just about anything, the inhabitants of Felicity-by-the-Lake shut them-selves in their houses at night, they avoided the silver lake at the south end of the village, and never in public did they utter a word against the mayor.

Daria

Together with the Hoyties in their great stone house lived Daria Smart, the twelve-year-old daughter of Mrs. Hoytie's second cousin once removed. Daria had been forced by the courts to live with the Hoyties after the death of her parents some years before, and had been dragged hither and yon as they careened from town to town.

Now that it was summer and school was out, Daria worked most every day, from dawn to dusk, at the specialty shop that Mr. and Mrs. Hoytie owned. Because her benefactors were lazy as well as greedy, selfish, and mean, they treated her as though she were their servant and had her do the bulk of the labor, and ever since Sam had become constable and had no time to help out at the shop, Daria had been busier than ever. Though Miss Edna Gagney was employed in the mornings as the baker and pastry chef, Daria was responsible for everything else. She opened the shop before the sun rose and closed it at six; she mopped the floors and washed the pots and pans; she mixed the hot chocolate, hand-dipped the bonbons, kneaded the bread, roasted the meat, waited on customers, made deliveries, cut the flour with cornstarch as Mr. Hoytie had taught her, and brought the strongbox home each evening to Mr. Hoytie's counting room.

And once she was home, she had to cook and serve the Hoyties dinner and clean the kitchen afterward. When she finally slept, it was in a stifling, coffin-sized room in the attic of the old stone house. Her life was hard, but she felt she had nowhere else to go, and though she didn't much like the Hoyties, she was grateful for the roof over her head.

Daria was slender and tall for her age, with arms and legs well muscled from all the work she had done for the Hoyties. Her hair was the light brown color of almonds, and her eyes were the speckled brown green of rocks seen through clear water in a stream. Not many people could look at her straight on, for her gaze was direct and unabashed. She had few friends, because she was new in town, and besides, who had time to make friends between working at home and working at the shop? Even if she had been free to play tag and statues and kickball, she wouldn't have been very popular, for she didn't much care for games.

Her best friend in the village was Anne Wilford, the daughter of Lyman and Betsy, and Daria surely would have voted for Mr. Wilford and not for Mr. Hoytie if she'd been old enough to vote. At least every other day, Anne came into the shop to visit Daria, and whenever she was finished with the book she was reading, Anne would lend it to Daria, and Daria would take it home to read by candlelight in her coffin-sized attic room. Daria knew that she and Anne had been destined to be close friends, because one could tell a lot about a person from the books she liked, and Daria loved the books that Anne loved and didn't much care for the ones to which Anne was indifferent.

The shop was closed on Sundays. Daria and Sam were required to accompany Mr. and Mrs.

Hoytie to church and to act like dutiful children; in fact, on Sundays Daria had been ordered to call Mr. Hoytie Poppa and Mrs. Hoytie Mummy, even though the rest of the week she was supposed to call them Mr. and Mrs. Hoytie. The Hoyties went to church because they believed it made them look virtuous, and besides, it gave them a chance to show off and smile benignly. They always dressed as if they were going to a fancy ball, and they always seemed annoyed that the other members of the congregation were not praying and singing hymns to *them*.

After the service, and after Mr. and Mrs. Hoytie stood outside the church door wringing the hands of all the villagers (whether the villagers wanted their hands wrung or not), Daria would rush back to the large stone house to cook a midday dinner, which Mr. and Mrs. Hoytie and Sam would eat with a great smacking of lips. And when she had cleaned the kitchen and straightened the house, she was finally free to go, and every Sunday afternoon she would walk to the house of Mr. and Mrs. Wilford to visit Anne.

Though she had this one friend, Daria spent so much time alone that she longed for a pet. But she wasn't allowed to have one (not even a rabbit or a parakeet), because Mrs. Hoytie was allergic to all animals on some days and on others she simply couldn't abide the mess made by fur and feathers. And so it was that Daria befriended Flumadiddle, who spent a fair amount of time at the shop because Miss Gagney worked there. From time to time Miss Gagney would stop rolling out dough or whipping buttercream to pick the cat up and pet her and say, over and over, "Oh, Flumsey, you are the most *beautiful* cat. Oh, I love you so *much*." And she would squeeze her and squeeze her until the cat gave a grating *meeeow*, at which Miss Gagney would put her down in embarrassment.

Though Flumadiddle did not like the squeezing, she rather liked the praise. All morning she would laze in the front window on a satin pillow Miss Gagney had brought from home, basking in the admiration of the villagers who would stop and look at her, curled in the sun, while behind her, in splendor, were stacked the loaves of bread and assorted pastries. When she woke from her naps, she would stretch, yawn, and slink to the kitchen, where Miss Gagney could be counted on for a special treat of one sort of another—a tidbit of chicken pâté or a scrap of smoked salmon or a saucer of fresh milk. And Daria spoiled her too, picking her up and scratching her between the

ears, while Miss Gagney looked on, her face twisted with possessiveness.

All three of them kept an eye open for the cat-hating Hoyties. According to them, cats were overgrown rodents, sly and sneaky and not to be trusted, who ruined the furniture and soiled the carpet and spread their hair everywhere. If there was even a hint of Hoytie in the air, Flumadiddle was gone without having to be told, and Daria sometimes wished she could do likewise.

Through Flumadiddle, Daria got to know Gigamaree, who was as lank and scruffy and skittish as his sister was fat, well groomed, and tolerant of people. Daria felt sorry for Gigamaree, who lived with a cranky and bad-tempered man. She thought if Gigamaree had had a Miss Gagney to dote on him, he might have been a very different sort of cat altogether.

One evening just before closing, Daria was mopping the kitchen floor. She had been alone all afternoon since Miss Gagney had left, and there hadn't been a single customer—business had fallen off alarmingly since the proclamations. She was looking forward to getting out of the shop, even if it meant merely returning home to serve the Hoyties dinner, when she heard a grating *meeeow* at the back door. She put down her mop and propped open the door to find Flumadiddle and Gigamaree both looking up at her expectantly. "Come in," she said. She stooped and petted them both. "Let me find you something."

All the food had been wrapped and put in the icebox, but Daria remembered the leg of lamb that she had roasted that morning. There could be no harm, she thought, in giving each of the cats a small sliver of meat. The cats twined themselves in and out of Daria's legs as she put the roast on the counter and carefully shaved off two slices. She had just dropped the meat to the floor when she heard a noise in the front of the shop and, startled, turned to see Mrs. Hoytie standing there. By the time she looked down, Flumadiddle and Gigamaree had fled out the back door, but not before Mrs. Hoytie had seen them.

"Daria," Mrs. Hoytie said, her voice fast, cold, and sharp, "were those cats I just saw?"

"I beg your pardon?" Daria said.

"Two cats? Did I just see two cats? Inside this shop? Don't lie to me, young lady."

"Two cats?"

"You wicked girl," Mrs. Hoytie cried, and almost before Daria knew what was happening, the woman had slapped her face.

"I hate cats," Mrs. Hoytie said. "Dirty creatures! They'd as soon put a run in a stocking as look at you, and they spread disease, oh yes they do. If I ever see a cat in this shop again, I shall . . . I don't know what I shall do, but mark my words, young lady, it will be nothing to look forward to. Did you touch them?"

"No, ma'am," Daria said. "I was just—"

"I don't care what you were doing so long as you never do it again," Mrs. Hoytie said, and she stamped her foot. "Now wash your hands with lye soap and stick them in boiling water. And then you finish cleaning up in here and get home as quickly as possible. I just dropped in to tell you to bring a loaf of bread and a bit of cheese when you come. Be quick about it." And before Daria could ask what kind of cheese she wanted, Mrs. Hoytie had swept out the door and into the street.

Daria finished mopping, her cheek still burning from the slap; then she took a loaf of French bread and a chunk of white cheddar, tucked the strongbox under one arm, and locked the door. She trudged up Orchard Street toward the spot on the edge of town where the immense stone house stood, and all the way she kicked a small pebble and wished it were Mrs. Hoytie.

Ulwazzer Returns

Since Ulwazzer belonged to no one in the town and had no proper home there, he'd always come and gone as he pleased, and not long before the mayoral election he had left Felicity-by-the-Lake for warmer realms, as he always did at that time of year. He had been to other towns beyond the mountains; he had seen the winter wheat grow tall in distant fields and had watched the fruit trees flower far from home. But now, at the beginning of June, he found he missed the lake at the foot of the jagged mountains and the town where he had been born, and so he returned.

At such a lovely time of year, it was impossible to imagine that all was not right with the world. The meadows surrounding Felicity-by-the-Lake were stippled with the bright dots of wild-flowers—the luscious purple and raspberry stalks of lupine, the white coronas of daisies, each holding at its center a miniature sun. At the edge of the village, ancient stands of lilac held forth their delicate white and lavender bouquets; hedges shone with pink five-petaled roses. The days were warm, and the sky's few clouds were stitched to the sky by the bright needles of swallows.

The smells of fresh dirt and windswept grass so intoxicated Ulwazzer that at first he hardly noticed that no one was swimming or diving or splashing or boating, and beyond that, the surface of the lake was extraordinarily calm for this time of year. As always, water lilies exploded in reds and creams, and trout leapt, catching the sun on their fishy tails, but the waves that usually eddied in the wake of ducks with their ducklings and geese with their goslings were nowhere to be seen.

This was very puzzling, for the lake was known far and wide as a perfect place to raise a family (if you were a waterfowl). Some of the ducks and geese and swans had lived there as long as Ulwazzer could remember. But where were they now?

Suddenly Ulwazzer heard a murmurous, indistinct burble of quacks, which seemed to be coming from the reedy marshes on the lake's western shore. He padded over there, curious and concerned. As he approached, the murmur grew clearer, and occasionally he could hear the blunt honk of a goose mixed with the quacks.

Ulwazzer crouched at the water's edge. As he peered and focused, he thought he could catch glimpses of white feathers behind the green curtain of marsh grass. Without warning, a slinky neck snaked through the grass, and Ulwazzer found himself being stared at, coldly, by a swan with whom he had been quite friendly not so many months before.

"Well," said the swan curtly. "I hadn't expected to see *you* around here again."

Of all the things the swan might have said, this struck Ulwazzer as the oddest. "And why not?" he said. "What would keep me away?"

"Given the current state of things, the better question is, what would bring you *back*?"

"Whatever do you mean?" Ulwazzer asked. "What's happened?"

"What's happened?" the swan echoed. "This lake is no longer safe for any of us, fish, fowl, or feline, and none of the townsfolk comes here anymore—unless you count *them*, which I, personally, do not. Everyone's wary, and we have to hide in the marsh, and—"

"Now, slow down," said Ulwazzer. "You're talking too fast."

"Of course I am," the swan retorted. "Who has time for a leisurely discussion about the end of the world?"

"But what's the cause of all this? And who do you mean by 'them'?"

Before answering, the swan cocked her head, listening for something, and then returned her cool gaze to Ulwazzer. "If you don't know, you'll find out soon enough," she said. "No time to prattle on."

Just as quickly as her head on its long neck had darted into sight, it withdrew, leaving Ulwazzer alone again on the lake's shore. He looked around, but everything was as it always had been, the lake shining in the morning sun, the marsh reeds playing their plangent music as the wind whistled through them.

Then all was quiet for what seemed a very long time. Ulwazzer decided to take a swim. He slipped into the lake and let himself drift on the morning's peace. The water was silk to his fur, and he gave up even trying to make sense of the swan's dire speech. Swans, after all, were high-strung and temperamental. He was sure she had exaggerated; and though the absence of people was puzzling, Ulwazzer decided there had to be *some* explanation.

From the corner of his eye, he caught a flash of movement and turned in the water to watch the approach of a black water snake. The snake slipped across the surface as if it were glass. Perhaps this languid fellow would be able to offer testimony to counter that of the hysterical swan. The snake's head rose slightly, its tongue flickering.

"Good morning," Ulwazzer said to the snake.

The snake said nothing, but its tongue continued to flick in and out, as though testing the temperature.

"I don't mean to bother you," Ulwazzer said, "but perhaps you can help me. I've just heard that in the last few months, the situation at the lake has changed a great deal. Is that your opinion?"

"The sssssituation at the lake is sssssatisfactory," the snake said, "sssspeaking for myssssself, as I am wont to do."

"Ah," said Ulwazzer. "I'm glad to hear it."

"But then, the mayor and his wife are not fond of eating sssssnake." Without another word, the creature whipped past Ulwazzer and was gone.

Now that *was a curious thing to say,* Ulwazzer

thought. But he'd barely had time to puzzle over the snake's meaning when out of the rushes appeared a drake; his iridescent emerald head was brilliant in the sun, his pale bill held high above the water. Ulwazzer was startled by the frightened glint in the drake's eye. "Here they come!" the drake warned. Then he reared back, unfolded his wings, and beat them frantically, all the while keeping one eye on the shore as if it were overrun with predators.

From the direction of town Ulwazzer heard a heavy thumping and a high, thin shriek of annoyance. He watched as there stumbled into view a large man—a very large man—balancing a rowboat upside down on top of his head, while the oars were wedged in his armpits. Behind him walked a woman wearing a wide-brimmed hat, from under which came the prating screech. And following those two, slumped under the burden of all she had to carry, came a slender, almond-haired girl.

What a threesome! *This*, Ulwazzer thought, bore watching.

Peaceableness and Quietude

Daria sighed and lowered the overstuffed duffel to the ground. Then she carefully set down the heavy hamper. Ahead of her, Mrs. Hoytie stood yelling at her son.

"Sam, put the boat in over there," she ordered.

Sam unlocked his elbows, and the oars fell at his feet. Still balancing the rowboat on top of his head, he walked into the lake, up to his knees, and lifted the heavy boat into the air.

"No, wait!" Mrs. Hoytie called. "Over there will be better."

Sam stopped, lowered the boat back onto his

head, and turned around to see where his mother was pointing.

"There! There!" she said, dismissively, with a flick of her wrist.

Sam staggered sideways several feet to his left and lifted the boat into the air once more.

"No, wait!" Mrs. Hoytie called again. "I was right the first time."

She certainly was tiresome, Daria thought. All day long Mrs. Hoytie knew *just* what she wanted—until she changed her mind, at which point she was quick to assert that she knew just what she wanted again. Daria had spent more hours than she could count being run ragged as Mrs. Hoytie decided she wanted the armchair in *this* corner, and then in *that* corner, and then upstairs, and then . . . no, it had been in the proper place to begin with.

Sam was tottering back toward his mother when he suddenly yowled and threw the boat forward. It sailed into the air and crashed down, making a wave that splattered all the way to Mrs. Hoytie's velvet slippers.

"You clumsy oaf," Mrs. Hoytie yelled. "Now look what you've done!"

But Sam didn't hear her, because he'd been flung headlong into the water himself. He came up dripping, smiling foolishly, a water lily hanging from his ear. "I kicked a rock," he said thickly. "It hurt my foot."

Daria laughed, causing Mrs. Hoytie to whirl around and snarl, "What's so funny, young lady? Are you laughing at my son?"

"N—No, ma'am," Daria stammered.

Mrs. Hoytie turned back to Sam. "Now get that boat and bring it over here. Be quick about it!"

Sam dragged the boat out onto the sand, dried it with a big towel, retrieved the oars, and then helped his mother in, as she lifted her flouncy pastel skirts. "The pillows, the pillows," she called to Daria, fluttering her fingers.

From the duffel bag Daria unloaded the lounging mattress, and the pillows, and the parasol. Then she hoisted over the boat's side the wicker hamper with its pots of moisturizing cream and its load of dainty morsels: caramels rolled in chocolate and covered with crushed pistachios; watercress and cream cheese sandwiches; candied pineapple. She got into the boat and seated herself on the hard wood floor. Then Sam slung in the duffel, which still held his rifles and fishing poles, and pushed the boat off the beach into the water.

He lifted one large wet foot and then the other, trying to figure how best to clamber aboard. Finally he just heaved his bulk over the stern, almost swamping the boat, which caused his mother to slap a hand to her heart and glare at him venomously. He shrugged and grinned, then settled down; he placed the oars in the oarlocks and rowed powerfully out to the very middle of the lake, where he stopped his efforts and let the boat drift.

This was Daria's signal to get out paper and a pen.

Mrs. Hoytie clasped her hands on her chest and sank back into her lounging pillows in a swoon of self-satisfaction. "Just rest for a moment, Sammy, before you start shooting. Let me think." She looked at Daria pointedly. "Are you ready, in case I come up with a thought or two worth saving?"

"Yes, ma'am," Daria said.

"Well, then," Mrs. Hoytie began, "let me see what is on my mind." She paused, squinted at the sky as though something might be written there, took a deep breath, and began to absentmindedly twiddle her thumbs. "Though it is *just* a bit warmer today than I would have it were *I* in control of the temperature, one really shouldn't complain, should one?" This was said to no one in particular, and no one in particular replied. "After all, it is a lovely day. Look at those clouds—just like little marshmallow fluffs." She seemed especially pleased with herself after this

association and wiggled happily on her cushions. "I am ever so glad that my husband had the foresight to forbid access to the lake, for it is much more calming not to hear shrieking children or the shouts of their most unpleasant parents."

"Yeah, Ma," Sam said. "But it *was* fun to go swimming."

"Swimming is a *sport*," Mrs. Hoytie said. "And you know I detest all sports. This peaceableness and quietude is much better."

"I bet you're a good swimmer, Ma," Sam said.

Mrs. Hoytie smiled coyly. "That may be so, Sammy dear. As you know, your mother is good at any number of things. But to swim one must get wet, and I quite dislike getting wet, except in my very own personal tub." She whipped the tablet away from Daria, raised her monocle to her eye, and peered at Daria's tidy handwriting. *Temperature*, Daria had written. *Marshmallow fluff. More calming. Shrieking children. Good swimmer. Personal tub.*

She handed the tablet back to Daria and let the monocle fall. "Daria, *dear*," she said. "Perhaps a bit more detail." Without further ado, she continued.

"As I was saying: How *splendid* to have the lake to myself. And how fortunate to have such a big strong son who can bring home dinner every night." She glanced at Sam, who smiled back stupidly. "I wonder what we ought to have this evening. We've had quite a lot of duck and goose recently," she said. "Perhaps we ought to have whooping crane, or blue-crested kingfisher. What would you make with whooping crane, Daria?"

"I . . . I have no idea," Daria said.

"Perhaps casserole-roasted whooping crane with turnips," Mrs. Hoytie mused. "But enough about food," she said, picking up a watercress and cream cheese sandwich. She nibbled away contentedly for some time, while Sam stared dumbly at the mountains and Daria watched the shadows of clouds playing upon the lake's surface. When Mrs. Hoytie had finished eating her sandwich, she picked up a piece of candied pineapple and studied it as though it were a map of the world.

"You must admit, Daria," she said, "that not every woman has a husband with the wisdom and the power to change the course of history in a provincial town like this one. Who says that politicians can't make a difference? What will my clever Jeremiah come up with next?"

What indeed? Daria thought. "You surely don't want me to answer that," she said.

"Of course not; that's what we call a rhetorical

question," Mrs. Hoytie said. She paused and flung back her head dramatically. "He could announce, for example, that from now on, the month of July won't be called July at all but will be known as the month of Prucilla." She clasped her hands and gazed adoringly at the looking-glass sky. "On the first of Prucilla, everyone must give me a flower. On the second of Prucilla, everyone must send me a letter. On the third of Prucilla—"

Daria cleared her throat. She knew that there were thirty-one days in July, and that, unless interrupted, Mrs. Hoytie would work her way through the entire calendar. "What else do you think Mr. Hoytie might come up with?"

"Don't interrupt me," Mrs. Hoytie said. "You scattered my thoughts." She pushed herself to a sitting position and glared at Daria, snatched the tablet away again and read, *big strong son, wisdom and power, July, month of Prucilla.*

"Excellent," she said. She settled back and prepared to begin again.

But Sam, restless at having to sit quietly for so long, picked up a rifle and began to level it at the marshes where the ducks and geese and swans huddled. "That was good, Ma," Sam said, his finger on the trigger.

"Why, thank you, Sam," Mrs. Hoytie said

brightly. "As you know, I happen to have a gift for profundity."

"Can we play the word game?" Sam asked.

"Of course," Mrs. Hoytie said. "I'm pleased to hear you're taking an interest in words. Just give me one, any one that comes into your head, and I'll think of a rhyme for it. Go on, now."

Though it had been his idea, Sam had not planned ahead, and his brain, which was not full of words at the best of times, suddenly went empty. He almost panicked, until he remembered what he was holding in his two enormous hands.

"Gun!" he exclaimed, flooded with relief.

"Fun!" Mrs. Hoytie shot back at him. "Another!"

"Oar," said Sam.

"Bore," Mrs. Hoytie said meaningfully. "Give me something harder, please. How about you, Daria? Perhaps you can do better than Sam."

Daria certainly hoped she could. Though she felt an odd kinship with Sam, who was ordered around by the Hoyties quite as much as she herself was, Daria knew she was much smarter than the big lout, and that she had managed to maintain her own sense of what was right and wrong while Sam had long since given up thinking for himself and just let his parents do his thinking for him.

As Mrs. Hoytie began to drum her fingers impatiently on the side of the boat, Daria thought about the past two weeks and how Sam had stalked the streets of the village, carrying person after person back to the house to be fined by the mayor. "Proclamation," she said mildly.

"Good!" Mrs. Hoytie answered. "Devastation. All right, Sammy. Shoot away!"

Gleefully, Sam raised his rifle, looked through the sight, and squeezed the trigger. The boom of the gun echoed off the jagged mountains and filled the lake's basin with a deadly roaring. From the marshes, a great noise erupted as a gaggle of ducks and geese flew into the air. Sam calmly followed them with his rifle and again squeezed the trigger. Again the lake and its surroundings boomed, and this time a duck fell straight down into the water.

"Dead," said Daria.

Mrs. Hoytie glanced at her but then turned back to watch the geese, who had become a ragged check mark in the sky. "Bed, fed, head."

"Yes," Daria said. "And don't forget *bled*." She looked at Mrs. Hoytie squarely. "And *dread*."

Mrs. Hoytie's cheeks flamed and her eyes were two sharp little pebbles. "Why, Daria," she said viciously, "that's very good. That's very good indeed. My dear, you bear watching."

6

Evening in the Village

Ulwazzer looked on in horror as the oversized man with enormous hands fired round after round of buckshot at the lake's waterfowl, not even bothering to retrieve all those he'd killed, and hooked trout after trout on his fishing lines, pulling them into the boat until the woman with the grating voice held her nose between two fingers and complained about the smell. Such meanness! Such waste!

After the last gunshot had echoed, after the rowboat had been returned to shore and its passengers had disappeared from view, Ulwazzer found out all he could about what had happened while he'd been away. He learned from the terrified ducks and geese who remained that the huge man was the new mayor's son, and that the pudgy woman was the new mayor's wife. He learned about the proclamations the new mayor had issued, but Ulwazzer still didn't understand why the villagers—who had always struck him as sensible people—obeyed them. He decided to look up his brother and sister to see what they could tell him.

That evening, as the sun dipped behind the mountains and the shadows faded into the general twilight, the children of the village begged and pleaded as they always did when they were called home, yelling, "Five more minutes! Just five more minutes!" But despite their entreaties, doors and windows were soon banged shut against the encroaching darkness, and the grim certainty of spending another night isolated inside their homes settled over the townspeople.

As Ulwazzer padded up Main Street, toward the central fountain and the bronze statue of Felicity-by-the-Lake's first mayor, he thought he had never seen the town so quiet. Here it was, the height of summer, and light still lingered, but the cider parlor was closed up tight, and the café tables held their upside-down café chairs, and the ice cream shop was dark. Though petunias and geraniums filled pots and window boxes, the houses behind them seemed colorless and drab. Ulwazzer continued past Lyman Wilford's printing shop, the place in all of Felicity-by-the-Lake where he felt most at home. In the small garden at the back of the house, he had often found a scrap of bread soaking in thick milk. Several times he had stayed long enough to allow Anne, the Wilfords' daughter, to pet him. But there was no sign of life at the house tonight.

And so he turned down the lane on which Mr. Mayapple lived in a squat brick hut surrounded by a chain-link fence with a KEEP OUT sign. Behind the fence the ground was clotted with rankweed and thistles. Ulwazzer leapt to the top of the fence, spied an open window in the back of the house, and gingerly made his way there. Without a sound, he jumped to the outside sill of the window and peered through. The room was dirty and crowded with boxes and trash.

Before Ulwazzer had even opened his mouth to call for Gigamaree, the cat slunk into view. Ulwazzer crouched without moving until his brother noticed him. The gray cat's head shot up and he gave a hiss of contempt as he flicked his crooked tail and narrowed his eyes. "You!" he snarled. "I certainly didn't expect *this* visit."

"Good evening, brother," Ulwazzer said. "I remember you used to enjoy a nightly prowl, but I see that even you are obeying the mayor's proclamation."

"What business is it of yours?" Gigamaree said. "I'm a simple law-abiding cat who—"

"Law-abiding?" Ulwazzer said with a laugh. "What's brought about that change?"

Gigamaree's eyes narrowed further at his brother's sarcasm. "I live my life perfectly well with no interference from you," he said. "Now be off before I fetch Mayapple. He'll demonstrate his rifle, with its twin barrels loaded."

Without another word, Ulwazzer jumped down, grimly shaking his head at Gigamaree's meanness. He didn't expect much more from his sister, but he walked several lanes over to where Miss Gagney's bungalow stood, and whispered through the cat door the name Flumadiddle.

Flumadiddle was nearby, nibbling tapioca pudding from a small plate Miss Gagney had set by the icebox, and when she heard her name she went to the cat door and gingerly stuck her face through. She had grown far too fat to use the door any longer, and was careful not to wedge her head.

"You!" she exclaimed when she saw who it

was. "You haven't been seen in these parts in months. And now, after dark!"

"Good evening, sister," Ulwazzer said. "You're looking . . . larger."

"Why, thank you," Flumadiddle said. She was extraordinarily vain about her size, and her green eyes, and her tufted ears, and spotted coat. She peered at Ulwazzer haughtily and asked, "What do you want?"

"Only the news," Ulwazzer said mildly, "as I've been traveling."

Flumadiddle regarded her brother with caution. "What exactly is it you wish to know?"

"There's this small matter," Ulwazzer said, "of the new mayor."

"The mayor and his wife do not like cats," Flumadiddle said. "*That* I can tell you without fear of contradiction."

"It appears there is much they don't like. I was at the lake today—"

"So you've been busy breaking *all* his proclamations," Flumadiddle said.

Ulwazzer ignored her. "The mayor's wife and son were there—"

"At the lake?" Flumadiddle said in astonishment. "What about the snapping turtles?"

"What snapping turtles?" Ulwazzer asked. "Everyone knows there aren't any snapping turtles in the lake."

"Ha!" Flumadiddle said. "And I suppose you'll tell me that there aren't any wolves in the mountains either."

"That's right," Ulwazzer said. "I've just crossed the mountains. There are no wolves there."

"But the mayor says differently," Flumadiddle said, "and he *is* the mayor. Why would he issue these proclamations if not for our protection?"

"For his own selfish reasons," Ulwazzer said. "That son of his was shooting ducks and catching trout—more than anyone could eat."

"I don't believe you," she said.

Ulwazzer shrugged. "Suit yourself," he said, then continued his inquiry. "There was a slender almond-haired girl with the mayor's wife and son—"

"Daria," Flumadiddle said. "A lovely child. She lives with the Hoyties and works in their shop. And she, I can tell you, does not share their prejudice against cats."

"I'm glad to hear that," Ulwazzer said.

"Now if you'll excuse me," said Flumadiddle, "you've interrupted my dinner."

"Stay awhile longer," Ulwazzer said. "I'd like to know—"

"Enough questions," Flumadiddle snapped. Abruptly she withdrew her oversized head, and the swinging steel plate of the cat door clanged shut behind her.

The incivility of his brother and sister angered Ulwazzer, but it was more or less what he'd expected. He would just have to find out for himself the rest of what he wanted to know. He padded silently up and down the streets, surprised not to see a single person who had been willing to venture outside. Surely not everyone in Felicity-by-the-Lake was as easily fooled as his sister; surely they didn't all suddenly believe in wolves and snapping turtles.

The first stars had punched through the evening sky when Ulwazzer heard a rhythmic *stomp stomp stomp*. He quickly slipped between a woodpile and a small whitewashed cottage, where he could remain hidden and still watch the road. Soon he saw a shivering oval of light dart through the darkness. And then, over the heavy tread of the *stomp stomp stomp,* he heard a bass voice mumble, "Anyone about? Better look out!"

Lumbering into view came the square-jawed, sad-eyed, thick-tongued, sausage-fingered giant of a man who had wrought havoc at the lake that afternoon. He stomped and he chanted, swinging his lantern wildly about. Then he suddenly stopped cold, extinguished his light, and began to tiptoe. He moved stealthily and in total silence for five minutes while Ulwazzer watched him.

Just as suddenly the creeping stopped, the lantern was relit, and the man resumed stomping. "Anyone about? Better look out!" And off he went.

Trying to keep the man in view, Ulwazzer slunk from shadow to shadow. The mayor's son stomped up one street and tiptoed down another; he huddled chanting under a streetlamp and then silently slipped through the darkness. He was faster than might be expected for someone his size, and sneaky, hiding behind buildings and peering around corners and from time to time trying to peek into the windows of houses. Ulwazzer thought he had seen all there was to see. But then, across Lake Street, he glimpsed old Lionel Penrose, who had slipped outside to admire the stars. Mr. Penrose was disturbing no one, surely, and hadn't even ventured into the street, but the mayor's son spied him during one of his creeps, and in a sudden rush he ran up behind him, grabbed him by the ankles, and jerked him into the air. Mr. Penrose uttered a loud grunt, and from inside the house, where his wife had been watching, came a shriek. "See?" she cried. "I told you it wasn't safe!"

But by then the mayor's son was in the street, holding Mr. Penrose upside down high above the paving stones. And swinging the old man like the clapper of a bell, he began his way to the outskirts of town where his father's house stood. Ulwazzer had to hurry to keep up.

Dinnertime

As Sam Hoytie made his way toward home, his mother and father were just sitting down to their evening meal. Sam had supped earlier, at the Wagon Wheel Roundup and Victual Parlor, as he did every day. That afternoon he had eaten almost three pounds of barbecued opossum. Daria, who would have starved to death had she not made herself something to eat at the shop, now stood awaiting her orders, while the dining room blazed with light from a silver candelabra. The table, with its bone china and cut crystal, glittered prettily. At one end sat Mr. Hoytie, who had exchanged his blue waistcoat for a velvet smoking jacket and silk cravat; at the other end Mrs. Hoytie sat, in a pale lime taffeta dress.

The Hoyties had finished their smothered trout appetizer and Daria was clearing the table when she heard a commotion at the front door, and Sam burst in, holding Mr. Lionel Penrose by the ankles. The old man sputtered and waved his arms; Daria could see he was having trouble breathing. Mrs. Hoytie folded her napkin and dropped it curtly on the table. She screwed up her face in displeasure. "Sammy," she said, "can't this wait?"

But the mayor rubbed his hands together, pushed back his chair, and stood. "Business waits for no man, Prucilla. Well, well. What have we here?"

"He was outside, Dad," Sam said.

"Was he?" said Mr. Hoytie. "Lionel Penrose, haven't you learned that being outside at night is bad for your health? Bring him in here." He gestured toward the counting room across the hall, and moved aside as Sam passed, carrying Mr. Penrose.

Daria well knew what would transpire; she'd heard it happen several times a day since the proclamations had first been issued. The mayor would tell Sam to put the culprit down; there'd be protestations of innocence, a quick conviction, and the levying of a fine; the mayor would dutifully record this in his ledger; and then Sam would again lift the villager by the ankles and return him to where he'd been found.

But this time Daria didn't listen to what was going on behind her because her attention was focused solely on the strange cat who had streaked in when Sam opened the door and who was even now crouched underneath the table. The cat lay perfectly still and seemed to blend into the smoky Persian carpet. Daria was sure that this was the first time an animal of any kind had been inside the Hoyties' house. She'd never seen this cat before in Felicity-by-the-Lake, and indeed had never seen any cat that looked like this one. His fur seemed to glow with an inner heat and then, in a flash, turned gray as smoke. Though she knew it was impolite to stare, she couldn't help it.

Mrs. Hoytie was drumming her fingers on the table. She picked up a shaker of salt and examined it. From time to time she threw a pointed look in the direction of the counting room, clearly hoping her husband would hurry up and return to dinner.

Then she noticed Daria. "What are *you* gazing at so intently?" she said. She lifted the tablecloth, took a swift look, saw nothing, and sat back up.

Daria blushed and tried not to glance at the cat again.

"You may bring the main course," Mrs. Hoytie said.

Daria slipped into the kitchen and grabbed the platter with the casserole-roasted whooping crane and braised turnips. She returned to the dining room just in time to see Sam and an upside-down Mr. Penrose leave the house, swiftly followed by the strange cat. Daria shook her head and wondered if perhaps she'd imagined the whole thing.

"Well, my little chocolate éclair," said Mr. Hoytie as he sat back down, "we're three doons richer."

"But the whooping crane is cold, I'm afraid," Mrs. Hoytie said petulantly.

"No, no," said Mr. Hoytie. He sawed away at the bony breast on his plate, took a large forkful, and stuffed it in his mouth. A curious expression spread across his face. Daria could see his jaws working but making little progress; she'd eaten a morsel of the meal Mrs. Hoytie had ordered, and knew the meat was stringy and tough and tasted more of fish than of fowl. "Mmm," he said. "Very tasty."

"I'm glad you like it, dear," his wife said. "Now, about my idea . . ."

Mr. Hoytie looked at his wife severely. "Prucilla, I do believe that this is the second time since we sat down to eat that you have mentioned your idea." Mrs. Hoytie blushed. "It's all well and good to be proud of one's ideas, my nutmeat, but one must understand that to everything there is a season and that when I am eating it is not the season for ideas."

"Yes, dear," Mrs. Hoytie said, narrowing her eyes. Then, suddenly and rather violently, she sneezed.

"Bless you," said Mr. Hoytie.

Mrs. Hoytie's eyes were watering. "It's almost as though there's been a . . . a *cat* in the house," she said, peering around suspiciously.

"Nonsense," said her husband.

And that was the extent of the dinner conversation. Though there was no speech, other sounds made their way to Daria's ears: the scritch and scratch of silverware on china, the slip and slap of lubricated lips, the sharp click of teeth. From time to time Mrs. Hoytie put down her knife and fork, wiggled on her seat cushion, and opened her mouth, but each time this happened, the raised eyebrows of Mr. Hoytie stopped her cold.

At last Mr. Hoytie swallowed his final mouthful and washed it down with a great draft of wine; he sighed contentedly and pushed himself back from the table. "Daria," he said. "Fetch the port and cigars for me, and a cup of tea for Mrs. Hoytie, would you?"

Daria cleared the table, then she brought into the dining room a silver tray on which sat a box of cigars, a decanter filled with port, a glass snifter, and a tepid cup of chamomile tea.

"Now, about that idea, my little spoonful of honey," Jeremiah Hoytie said. He clipped the end of his cigar, sniffed it, smiled appreciatively, and lit it, then sucked deeply and sent into the room a noxious cloud of smoke. He poured himself a generous snifter of port and sat back in his chair, resting the glass on his round belly.

Mrs. Hoytie took a very deep breath and cleared her throat. Though her initial tone was cross, she quickly warmed to her task. "Well!" she began. "On the way down to the lake this morning, we crossed a meadow just *full* of flowers, with butterflies darting here and there. And birds were everywhere—not just the geese and ducks and whooping crane which Sammy shot, but other birds too; doves and robins and swallows. And I wondered, *Now, who do all those things belong to?*"

"Why, no one, my sweet. They're just *wild.*"

"But is that good?" Mrs. Hoytie asked. "Wouldn't it be better for them if they weren't so . . . so unrestrained?"

"Perhaps," Mr. Hoytie said.

"I want them," Mrs. Hoytie declared, her voice rising. "If no one owns them, why can't I have them?"

"My brilliant nonpareil," said Mr. Hoytie, opening his eyes wide. He inhaled and then released a great puff of smoke. "As you know, I have long been in favor of ownership."

"And I wondered about those mountains, and what might be under them," Mrs. Hoytie continued. "Do you know who owns them?"

"I don't," her husband said. "That will take some looking into."

From her corner, Daria stared at the two of them, slack-jawed with astonishment. It was almost as though she'd just witnessed a three-toed tree sloth composing a shopping list.

"I don't know if I'm making myself clear," said Mrs. Hoytie.

"Oh, but you are, my strawberry tart," Mr. Hoytie said. "As clear as the water in the lake. I see absolutely no reason why we should not own all the things you mentioned, and a good bit else besides. I will issue a new proclamation."

Mr. Hoytie jumped to his feet. He raised his snifter and cried, "To us!" and then snapped back his neck and drained the glass. "Prucilla, come with me."

"With pleasure," Mrs. Hoytie said. Her face was flushed with anticipation. "Daria, be a good girl and clean up this mess, won't you?"

Daria watched as Mrs. Hoytie took the crook of her husband's arm and allowed him to lead her from the dining room to his counting room, from which all proclamations issued.

CHAPTER 8

A New Proclamation and a New Alliance

Mr. Hoytie sat at his chestnut table, dipped the quill of his goose-feather pen into a vial of mirkberry ink, and began carefully to trace the letters on a piece of vellum. *Proclamation the Fourth*, he wrote in his peculiar curlicued hand, *From this day forward, anything which does not belong to you belongs to Prucilla and Jeremiah Hoytie*. It was cold in the counting room and Prucilla shivered, though whether this was because of the temperature or her pleasure, her husband could not tell.

"Beautifully worded," said Prucilla Hoytie. "A masterpiece of economy."

The mayor nodded benignly. "Thank you, my precious candied yam," he said. "I have half a mind to dedicate this proclamation to you. Now if only Sam were still here, he could take it round to the printer."

"Why, we can send Daria!" Mrs. Hoytie said. "She can finish the dinner dishes later. Finding Sam should be easy enough for her. Those boots of his make plenty of noise when he's stomping."

"Another splendid idea," Mr. Hoytie said, and together they strode into the kitchen.

"Daria," Mrs. Hoytie said, "you're to stop that immediately and go find Sam."

"Now?" said Daria, turning. Her hands dripped soapy water.

"Yes, now," Mrs. Hoytie said. "We have something we want you to give him."

"Here," Mr. Hoytie said, waving a dish towel in Daria's face. "Dry those hands." And when that had been accomplished, the mayor brandished the piece of vellum. "Deliver this to Sam and tell him to take it round to the printing shop for immediate duplication and distribution."

"Tonight?" Daria asked.

"Tonight!" Mr. Hoytie thundered. "Do you have potatoes in your ears?"

"No, sir," Daria said. She pulled off her apron,

folded the piece of paper in half, and began to tuck it into her pocket.

"Now don't lose that," Mrs. Hoytie warned. "That's a very important proclamation."

Daria groaned. "Another one?"

"Young lady," the mayor said, "I take that very amiss. I find myself disappointed in you to a high degree. I am the mayor of Felicity-by-the-Lake and it is part of my duty to issue proclamations; that is what the good people of this little burg elected me to do. You, on the other hand, are an orphan without support in this world, a burden on the common weal, and Mrs. Hoytie and I took you in out of the goodness of our hearts. This is how you repay us? Now hurry it up and find Sam."

The next thing Daria knew, she was out the door and standing in the dark. The sudden turn of events had left her shaking her head in disbelief. Here she was, outside! She hadn't been outside after the Hoyties' evening meal since the first proclamation had been issued in April, and she was interested to see what things were like.

She knew that she'd see no wolves, and, frankly, this disappointed her; she understood that Mr. Hoytie had made them up to terrify the townsfolk, and she was flabbergasted that he'd succeeded. She remembered the way he had leapt at her with his fingers curled and his face contorted when he described the gray and nasty wolves with their sharp white fangs and pointed snouts who padded down from the mountains each and every night to eat the people of Felicity-by-the-Lake, and she knew right then that the town had far more to fear from him than from any pack of wolves.

She took a deep breath and listened. Sure enough, in the distance she heard the rattle of window glass and the heavy *stomp stomp stomp* of boots, poor Sam's attempt to frighten off the imaginary wolves he himself was so afraid of. She set off in that direction.

Daria was amazed at how dark and silent Felicity-by-the-Lake was. Not a single light gleamed behind a curtained window. In the days of spring before the proclamations, the village had been filled with the festive sounds of neighbor calling to neighbor, of children playing with one another (if not with her), of cats and dogs running free. Daria's great regret was that she didn't feel as fully a part of life here as she would have liked; ever since Mr. Hoytie had begun issuing proclamations, most of the people of the town had been short with her, and their children had gone out of their way to avoid her.

Tonight it seemed she walked through a ghost town—the houses were each as dark and still as a rectangle of slate, and nothing moved in the streets or behind the bushes. It was as though every mouse, every owl, every bat, every mosquito had holed up in deference to the mayor's proclamation.

The air was cool, and it carried with it the fragrance of lake water. In front of Daria the mountains rose high and wide, a single black mass, blotting out the stars, while everywhere else the sky was so powdered with light that it seemed to pulse. Daria wished there really *were* wolves in the mountains. She hurried her pace, rounded a corner, and heard Sam's mournful keen. "Anyone about? Better look out!" Then there was a *stomp stomp stomp* and a repeat of the warning.

"Sam!" Daria called.

Sam froze in his tracks and drew himself up to his full seven-foot height, all two hundred and eighty-seven pounds of him. He looked around in fury. "Who's there?" he called. "Who is it?"

But before Daria could get her name out, Sam had thundered up, bent over, grabbed her ankles, and hauled her off her feet. Hanging upside

down, the blood banging in her ears, Daria stared into Sam's massive kneecaps.

"Sam, it's me!" Daria shouted. "Put . . . me . . . down!" She pummeled Sam's knees with her fists.

"Huh?" Sam said.

"It's Daria!" Daria shouted.

All of a sudden Daria felt herself being turned right side up and drawn in close to Sam's face. "Daria!" Sam finally exclaimed. "What are you doing here?"

As she was being lowered to the ground, dizzy and sick to her stomach, Daria said, "Your father sent me. He wanted me to give you this." She handed Sam the piece of folded vellum. "It's another proclamation."

Sam squinted at the paper. "Another proclamation," he said reverently. He held it out in front of him, then brought it close to his eyes. Daria knew Sam couldn't read but that he was embarrassed to say so. "I better get this to the printer," he said. "You want to come?" He smiled foolishly at her and blushed.

Daria's head was still spinning. "No," she said. Going to the Wilfords' with a proclamation? She didn't think so. "No, thanks."

But Sam didn't move; he just stood there staring at Daria, his ham-fisted hands hanging at the ends of his long meaty arms. The silence began to make her so uncomfortable she decided to retaliate.

"Have you seen any wolves?" she asked, knowing this would frighten him.

A look of panic crossed Sam's face, and he instantly spun around. "Wolves?" he said. "Where? Where are they? Where?"

"I haven't seen any," Daria said. "I just wondered if *you* had."

"No," Sam said, vastly relieved. "And I don't want to. I'm scared of wolves." The look on his face was so piteous that Daria reached out and patted his arm.

"Well," she said, "you better get going."

"OK," Sam said brightly. "But keep your eyes open. If you see anyone breaking the law, you just give a holler." Then he ran off toward Mr. Wilford's street. As he went, the *stomp stomp stomp* of his boots was even more earthshaking than usual.

Sam got to the print shop all out of breath; he wheezed as he pounded on the wood-slat door. Boards shrieked as their nails pulled loose. When at last the frousled and grumpy printer stood before him, Sam thrust at the man the vellum Daria had given him.

"My father wants one hundred copies of this proclamation," he said.

"Another proclamation!" Lyman Wilford bellowed. "Is there no end to this? Can't it wait until morning?"

"He wants them now," Sam said.

"In the middle of the night?"

"Now," Sam said.

Lyman Wilford unfolded the paper. " 'Proclamation the Fourth,' " he read. " 'From this day forward, anything which does not belong to you belongs to Prucilla and Jeremiah Hoytie.' " He began to laugh.

"What's so funny?" Sam demanded.

"Why, this is ridiculous," Mr. Wilford said. "Your father has gone right over the edge. Where does he get these things?"

Sam pointed to his oversized, square-jawed head. "From his brain," he said. "That's why he's the mayor."

"But surely even *you* can see how idiotic—"

"*Now!*" thundered Sam, and he bashed the door so hard with his fist that a board in the middle broke in two, and Lyman Wilford jumped back.

"It'll be a while," Mr. Wilford said. "Why don't you get on with your important work of terrorizing the town and leave me alone to print this?"

"OK," Sam said.

Daria quickly walked home the way she had come. Still dizzy from having been held upside down and shaken, she found herself staggering from one side of the road to the other, the way she'd seen Sam behave one night when he'd drunk a barrelful of cider. She did nothing but put one foot in front of the other, until she heard a rustling in the barberry hedge at the front of the Bullocks' property.

In an instant, her head had cleared. "Who's there?" she called, her voice cautious but strong. The rustling ceased. Daria had backed up two steps and then another two when there emerged from the barberry hedge the cat she had seen earlier that evening, under the Hoyties' dining table. It was a cat with amber eyes and fur the color of burning leaves. And when the evening wind touched the cat's coat, it glowed and dimmed as embers would, first smoldering, then fading to the cool gray of ash. Daria stood transfixed as the cat slipped up to her and began to twine itself in and out of her legs.

She thought she knew all of the animals who lived in Felicity-by-the-Lake, but this cat was a stranger to her. "Where did you come from?" she asked in wonder.

The cat sat before Daria, glancing up at her. He fixed her with his eyes as if inviting her to talk, but she was too amazed to know what to say. After a time the cat stretched, yawned, and began to wash his face, and Daria was suddenly aware that she didn't want to be ignored. She knelt down and stretched a hand toward the cat. "I saw you earlier," she said. "In the mayor's house."

The cat looked up at Daria amiably, as though to say, *And I saw you, too.* And then he moved forward until his back was under her outstretched hand. Daria stroked the cat's strange fur, so alive under her fingers; it was the softest fur she'd ever felt. "I wish you were mine," she said.

The cat shook his head as if to tell her this could never be, and Daria sadly thought that no matter how much she wished for it, he was probably right. "I've always wanted a cat," she said, "but those people I live with . . . well, they don't like them." Instantly the cat arched his back; his eyes, which had been open so wide, had closed to slits.

"It's all right," Daria said. "I wouldn't let them hurt you. Now, let's see who you *do* belong to." All cats and dogs in Felicity-by-the-Lake were required to wear collars embroidered with the names of their owners. But as Daria's hand passed over the cat's neck, she was surprised to discover that it was bare. He wore no collar. Had he been lost? Or was this really a cat without a place to live? She looked at him closely as if he might tell her, but of course he did not. "Then why don't you come home with me?" she asked. "I'll sneak you in."

She scratched behind the cat's ears, and he closed his eyes in bliss. She wished she had a tidbit of something in her pocket for him. When she stopped scratching, the cat pressed his head against her hand, as if asking for more.

Daria remembered the day she'd been caught feeding Flumadiddle and Gigamaree at the specialty shop; she remembered the cold look in Mrs. Hoytie's eyes and the hot sting of the woman's slap. How much worse it would be if Mrs. Hoytie found her sneaking a cat into the house!

"I don't care," she said aloud, and she picked the strange cat up in her arms and began to walk toward the Hoyties' immense stone house. But she hadn't gotten more than a few feet before the cat wrestled free of her arms and jumped to the ground. At first Daria was almost frightened by how fiercely he had resisted being held, and wondered if he would now scratch her or bite her. But as she stood there, her heart beating, the cat came and rubbed himself against her ankle again, and Daria decided he was simply cautious and didn't like to be held.

"Come on, then," she said. "You'll have to follow me." And she strode off, with the cat trotting beside her as if he'd always been there.

In the Mayor's House

Though Ulwazzer had little reason to trust his sister about most things, he could see that Flumadiddle had been right about Daria; she was a lovely girl, and she seemed to be very fond of cats. And he admired the fact that she hadn't attempted to pick him up again after he'd jumped from her arms. Ulwazzer knew that most people would have been made angry by his jumping down as he had and would have tried to exert their dominance—he'd seen it many times. But this girl seemed different from most people. When the mayor's house came into view, Ulwazzer's ears perked. Before, when he had followed the mayor's son, he'd gotten no farther than the rug under the dining room table. Now his good fortune would allow him greater access: he would see what he could discover.

Daria mounted the stone steps and grabbed the door's handle. "Oh, no!" she muttered, and Ulwazzer understood from the way her shoulders slumped that the door was locked and she had no key. She shook her head in what seemed a little flurry of anger, took a deep breath, closed her eyes, and then she knocked, and knocked again, and altogether Ulwazzer thought the two of them had been standing outside the door for close to ten minutes before the high whining voice of the mayor's wife filtered through the keyhole.

"Who is it?" Mrs. Hoytie asked. Ulwazzer crouched beside the stone steps under a hydrangea.

"It's Daria, Mrs. Hoytie," Daria called.

There was the sound of the dead bolt turning, and the chain being undone, and then the door was flung open. "It's about time," Mrs. Hoytie said. "Where have you been?" A hand reached out, grabbed Daria by the arm, and yanked her inside. Without further ado, the door slammed shut, the dead bolt turned, and the chain rattled.

Ulwazzer didn't let this bother him; he stayed crouched where he was while the voices on the other side of the door rose and fell. "Did you find Sammy?" Mrs. Hoytie asked.

"Yes, I—"

"And did you give him the proclamation?"

"Yes, I—"

"And what took you so long? If you'd been another ten minutes, Mr. Hoytie and I would have gone to bed and left you outside for the wolves to eat."

Daria smiled grimly at how hard the Hoyties were trying.

"Well, you're a lucky girl indeed," Mrs. Hoytie said. "Now I'm off for my beauty rest. Make sure you clean up the kitchen before you go to bed. I expect to see it spotless in the morning."

"Yes, Mrs. Hoytie," Daria said.

And then there was silence.

Ulwazzer didn't move, and sure enough, after a few minutes, the dead bolt clicked, the chain whispered, and the front door creaked open. Daria stood there, with her finger in front of her lips. "Come in," she whispered. "Be as quiet as you can."

Daria secretively closed and relocked the door. The lamps had been extinguished and the candles snuffed; the entry and living room were dark except for the rectangular glimmer of moon that lay across the floor like a carpet of light. Ulwazzer followed Daria to the kitchen, where he watched her strike a match and light the wicks of the two oil lamps on the table. As a mountain of pots and dishes and glasses arose out of the darkness, Ulwazzer noticed the weary expression that clouded Daria's features for a brief moment.

"Are you hungry?" Daria asked him. She went to the icebox and took out a small bottle of heavy cream, then poured it into a shallow bowl and tore up some scraps of bread to soak in it. Ulwazzer purred, and he rubbed himself against her hand as she put the dish on the floor. While he ate, he listened to the sounds of her toil—the scraping and stacking of plates, the organizing of glassware, the separating of silver. Then he heard her sigh ever so slightly as she poured water from a pitcher into the sink and began to scrub away.

Criminal Mischief

When a reasonable time had passed, Sam returned to Lyman Wilford's house and print shop. The first posters were now dry enough to hang, and so Sam did as he'd done before—he began nailing and pasting them in conspicuous places, on kiosks and brick walls and abandoned doorways. Some of the earlier proclamations were still in place, though Sam was disconcerted to discover that many had been shredded or otherwise defaced. One was decorated with crude cartoons of his father and mother; another was splattered with yellow paint. Several had been scrawled upon with charcoal. A copy of Proclamation the First had been carefully altered to read *"Wall musk begin their mouses by darn."* Sam squinted at it for quite some time but still could make no sense of it.

Villagers long asleep were now rudely awakened by Sam's banging and hammering. As they peered through cracks in their shutters and blinds, as they peeked through keyholes and from behind curtains, they could see the large heading, *Proclamation the Fourth,* but in the dim light they couldn't make out the rest.

When Sam blundered off to post a new copy, Caleb Withers, a young man of fourteen who held the village record for the mile run and who took great pride in his superior speed, darted over to read the new official utterance. So absurd did Caleb think it that he burst into laughter, and in no time Sam had thundered back and yanked him off the ground.

"No one is allowed outside after dark!" Sam yelled.

"Put me down, you gigantic oaf," yelled Caleb Withers, trying to push his nightshirt off his face and back up over his undergarments. But Sam was happily on his way.

* * *

The capture did not go unobserved. Gigamaree leapt up to the windowsill and yowled until the irascible Mr. Mayapple hurled a shoe and roared at him to shut up and go back to sleep. So Gigamaree shut up, but he stayed where he was long after the echo of Sam's voice had disappeared. He crouched, tail twitching, eyes narrowed to yellow slits, looking for all the world as if he were finally falling asleep, but in fact he was thinking mean thoughts and peering out at the darkness.

Even now he imagined the mice and voles who were running everywhere, at ease, without his pouncing expertise to keep them in check. Why, they were probably eating Felicity-by-the-Lake from the ground up! To make matters worse, he remembered his earlier encounter with his long-gone brother Ulwazzer. The more he thought about it, the more outraged Gigamaree became. Here he was, a true citizen of Felicity-by-the-Lake, forbidden to wander the streets of his own village at night. And yet this outcast, this trespasser, did just as he pleased, without the rude intervention of the ham-sized hands of Sam.

Staring out at the night, Gigamaree idly wondered how he could keep his brother from enjoying the pleasures he himself was denied—or at least get him punished. Then the thought occurred to him to consult with Flumadiddle, who, though lazy and vain, was generally good with ideas. Emboldened by the certain knowledge that Sam was on his way to the mayor's house with his latest victim, Gigamaree decided to sneak over to Miss Gagney's. The flimsy ripped curtains of Mr. Mayapple's pantry floated in the evening breeze, and Gigamaree leapt to the ground and began to make his way several streets over to where his sister lived.

He stuck his head in the cat door and found Flumadiddle asleep, curled on the hearthrug. Soundlessly he slipped inside and whispered his sister's name. She roused with a start and almost bounded into the air.

"What are *you* doing here in the dead of night?" she growled. Her eyes blazed.

"I need your help," Gigamaree said. "You're always better with plans and ideas than I am."

This placated Flumadiddle almost instantly, for she had a robust appreciation of her own intelligence. "Well," she said as she calmed down and began to lick her electrified fur. "Thank you. What can I do?"

"Ulwazzer's back," Gigamaree said. "He had the nerve to jump up on Mayapple's pantry windowsill earlier tonight."

"He came to visit me, too," Flumadiddle said.

"Did he?" Gigamaree said. "Then you know exactly what I'm talking about. Mind you, it was almost dark, and no one is allowed outside after dark."

"Yes, I know," Flumadiddle said mildly. "Quite so. But he has no house to go to."

"That's no excuse," Gigamaree said, scowling. "He shouldn't be in town in the first place. He's not wanted here."

"Indeed not," said Flumadiddle. "But I don't see what that has to do with us."

"How do we turn him in?" Gigamaree asked. "I want to see him punished. I want to see him dangling from that lummox's hands."

Flumadiddle's eyes widened. Though she was fond of Gigamaree, she had to admit he had his vicious side. "He *is* our brother," she reminded him gently.

"So what?" Gigamaree said. "Why should he be allowed to roam around at night if I can't?"

"I see what you mean," said Flumadiddle, although she didn't, quite. "Nevertheless, it would be easier all around just to forget about it. Out of sight, out of mind."

"I don't want to forget about it," Gigamaree said.

Flumadiddle yawned. Clearly her brother was

not about to give up, and she saw that her own interest in getting back to sleep wouldn't be satisfied until she came up with an idea for him.

"Let me think," she said. She closed her eyes and thought, and thought some more, letting the ideas flit by as though they were moths or mayflies. And then it came to her. Her eyes shot open. "You could write an anonymous note," she said, "telling the mayor about this cat who breaks all the proclamations. Describe Ulwazzer and suggest that the mayor send that oversized meat loaf to track him down."

"Brilliant!" Gigamaree said. "But *you'll* have to write it; you know how bad I am with my letters."

And so Flumadiddle jumped to the top of Miss Gagney's escritoire, flopped open the mahogany lid, and uncorked the bottle of India ink. She pulled out a sheet of highly perfumed stationery, dipped a fine-nibbed pen in the ink, and in large scratchy letters began relaying the tale of the cat with fur the color of burning leaves and fur the color of smoke, a cat who wandered at will and never stayed inside after dark and undoubtedly roamed by the lake as well and who spent all his time criticizing the mayor.

Flumadiddle was very pleased with her result,

and after blotting the ink with her tail, she jumped back to the floor and handed the paper to her brother. "There," she said. "All you need to do is slip this under the mayor's front door."

"I knew I could count on you," Gigamaree said. "Now go back to sleep, and I wish you most pleasant dreams. I'll see you tomorrow." He slipped through the cat door and was gone.

11

Behind the Curtain

Ulwazzer wasn't used to such rich fare as the cream and bread that Daria had given him, so he could only eat half. He turned and observed Daria as she went about her cleaning. Though her shoulders sagged unhappily, her back was strong. She made quick work of the pots and hung them, one by one, from their hooks in the ceiling.

As she started in on the dishes, Ulwazzer decided to see what he could find out about this mayor and his plans. He slipped back into the dining room, and then across the hall to the mayor's counting room. Rumbling down the stairs came the stentorious sound of the Hoyties' snoring. On the floor behind the desk stood a large wooden trunk wound round with heavy chains and padlocked with a formidable array of locks. There was no way of telling how many doons lay within, but Ulwazzer was sure it was a treasure's worth. Jumping up on the mayor's desk, he found a leather-bound ledger on top of a blotter. He flipped open the cover and scanned the entries, pages and pages of them: the names of villager after villager and the fines they'd been forced to pay.

When he had reached the last page, Ulwazzer nudged the ledger out of the way. Underneath it, on top of the blotter, he discovered the drafts and scratchings of new proclamations the mayor was thinking of instituting.

> From this day forward, Felicity-by-the-Lake shall be known as Hoytie-by-the-Lake.

> ~~From this day forth~~ Beginning now on, ~~the month of~~ July will be ~~known as the month of~~ called Prucilla.

> August = Jeremiah (?) Prucilla & J addressed as "Your Excellencies."

All dogs on leashes at all times.

All cats banned from Hoytie-by-the-Lake. By the First of Jeremiah? Cat owners who do not get rid of their cats fined ~~one hundred~~ five hundred doons.

All families allowed one child. All extra children belong to the Hoyties (for cooking, cleaning, street-sweeping, gardening, et cetera).

Outside the house, there was a sudden tumult—the *stomp stomp stomp* of heavy boots, the thin strained voice of a young man arguing, and then a hefty pounding at the door. Ulwazzer grabbed the piece of paper with the mayor's scribblings in his teeth and quickly darted behind some draperies, well out of sight.

In his dream, the mayor had been seated on a huge gold throne, and he was exceedingly grumpy as he shuffled to the front door. He thought, as he reached for the knob, that he would have to instruct Sam to stop bringing people round in the middle of the night. Though business *was* business, he needed his sleep.

He wore a pair of silk pajama bottoms cinched around his enormous belly by a length of braided cord; from this belt hung the keys to the locks guarding the trunk in his counting room. Over his chest he had hastily pulled his blue waistcoat with the brass buttons, and from his head dangled his tasseled nightcap.

Mayor Hoytie pulled open the door with a grunt. There stood his son and heir, holding by the ankles the twisting and gyrating figure of fourteen-year-old Caleb Withers.

"Well, well, what have we here?" Mayor Hoytie said.

"Mayor Hoytie," began Caleb Withers, "you can't do—"

"Young Master Withers," said Jeremiah Hoytie, "good evening. Sammy, you know where to take him."

Sam passed his father, and as he did, Caleb Withers extended a flailing arm to grab the mayor, but Mr. Hoytie sidestepped nicely. He followed Sam into the counting room, and when Sam stood still, holding the jerking boy, Mr. Hoytie sat down at his desk, briskly lit the oil lamp, and reached forward to flip open his leatherbound ledger. His blotter was empty.

"Put me down!" yelled Caleb Withers.

Mayor Hoytie remembered quite well that before he had followed his wife upstairs to bed, he had sat at this very desk, as was his wont, and looked casually over his ledger's pages. Then he had squared the ledger on the blotter. But it wasn't where he'd left it; in fact, it had been moved to the side of the desk. And where were the drafts he'd been working on?

"Sammy," he said, "were you in here, in this room, at any time this evening?"

"N-No, Dad," Sam said.

"Put me down!" yelled Caleb Withers again.

"Well, who was?" Mr. Hoytie asked.

"Maybe it was Ma," Sam said.

"It was not your mother; I know where your mother is at all times, and she was not in the counting room."

"Who else could it be?" Sam said. "Not Daria."

"That girl!" yelled the mayor. His face reddened, and his lips twisted, and his hands made fists on the desk. "If I find out that she was in here . . ."

"I bet she was dusting," Sam said helpfully.

Mr. Hoytie took a deep breath and thought of all the means by which he might inflict punishment on that thin slip of a child. "Anyway," he said, "business before pleasure."

"Put me down!" yelled Caleb Withers for the third time.

"You may do that, Sam," the mayor instructed.

And Sam dropped Caleb Withers on his head.

The boy rose from the floor, rubbing his crown. Mr. Hoytie growled, "And what is it you've been up to, if I may be so bold as to ask?"

"Nothing," Caleb said. "I was just—"

"Silence!" yelled the mayor.

"He was outside reading the new proclamation," Sam informed his father.

"Although that is in some respects commendable, you are old enough to know that *no one is allowed outside after dark!* Tomorrow would have been soon enough, Caleb. Your fine will be three doons."

Laboriously Mayor Hoytie wrote in his leatherbound ledger, *C. Withers. Procl. # 1. 3 d.* "Thank you very *much*." He stood and brandished his ring of keys, but was suddenly taken over by a tremendous yawn and said, "As you can see, the treasury is closed for the night. Therefore, your fine is payable by noon tomorrow." He was about to order Caleb Withers's return when Sam interrupted him.

"I still didn't see any wolves, Dad," Sam said.

Mr. Hoytie gaped at the enormous stupidity of

his son. He couldn't very well reassure him that there were no wolves in front of Caleb Withers.

"Excellent," Mr. Hoytie said. "Then the towns-people are doubly safe."

"I'm scared of wolves," Sam said.

"Be that as it may," Mr. Hoytie said sharply, "you will please take this boy back."

Sam reached down, grabbed Caleb Withers's ankles, and whisked him off the floor. Caleb sputtered and twitched, and raised an upside-down fist to shake in the mayor's direction.

"Tsk, tsk, tsk. No criticizing the mayor," Mr. Hoytie said. "And Sammy?"

"Yeah, Dad?"

"You may hulk around all you wish for the remainder of the night, but don't bring anyone else back here. I need to get my sleep."

"What should I do with them?"

"I don't care," Mr. Hoytie said. "You may do with them whatever you wish. Now good night."

CHAPTER

12

Banished

As the door banged behind Sam, Mr. Hoytie closed the ledger and squared it on the blotter. He thought about the ungrateful, selfish, utterly cavalier behavior of the young girl he and his wife had rescued from an uncertain fate. She had been without a home in the world, and they had opened their arms and welcomed her into the bosom of Hoytieness. They had given her a roof over her head and food if she needed it, and all the air she cared to breathe, and what had she done in return? Sure, she had cleaned their house several thousand times and served them their dinner; she had worked in their shop. But that did not begin to repay them for their loving generosity. And now she had had the temerity to enter the counting room? To move the ledger?

Mr. Hoytie could feel his temperature rising; his face, which was normally red as a sockeye salmon fillet, passed beyond red and became crimson, with shadings of purple. His beard began to tremble. On the desk before him, his fists were clenched so tightly that all blood had fled from his hands.

"Daria!" he yelled. "Daaaaa-reeeee-aaaaa!"

Long before her name was called, Daria had noticed that the cat was no longer in the kitchen with her. She had stood with her hands in hot water, her heart pounding in her chest. What if Mrs. Hoytie found the cat or—worse—if the cat found Mrs. Hoytie? Surely Mrs. Hoytie would figure out who had let the animal into the house. Where could he have gone? But perhaps he'd had the good sense never to have gone upstairs in the first place. And Mr. and Mrs. Hoytie *were* sound sleepers.

Daria had been about to mount a search when she heard banging at the front door and Mr. Hoytie's heavy footfalls on the stairs, and realized that Sam had brought home another villager for the ritual condemnation. She had finished up the dishes as quickly as she could, hoping that Mr. Hoytie would levy his fine and go back to bed before anything bad happened.

But she realized that the worst had come to pass when she heard the bellow of her name.

Daria rushed to the doorway of the counting room, wiping her hands on a dishcloth. Mr. Hoytie was sitting squarely at his desk. "There you are!" he yelled. "What have you been up to?"

Daria had no idea what he could mean, other than sneaking a cat into the house. "Excuse me, sir?" she said in her most obliging voice. "I've just been cleaning up the kitchen."

Mr. Hoytie rose and crossed his arms over his brass buttons. "Have you been in the counting room this evening?" he asked.

"No, sir," Daria said.

"Don't lie to me!" the mayor screeched. "First you come in here without my permission and then you deliberately evade the truth."

His refusal to believe her made Daria very angry. "I'm not lying," she said. "I haven't been in your room."

The mayor stared at her. "When haven't you been in my room?"

"I *always* haven't been in your room," Daria said.

"Well, someone has," Mr. Hoytie said. His voice grew low and menacing. "When I went to bed this evening, my ledger was in the middle of my blotter, and when I came downstairs, someone had moved it. Unless you're going to suggest to me that it moved by itself."

Daria understood who must have moved it, but of course she said nothing.

"Do you think it moved by itself?" the mayor asked haughtily.

"No, sir," Daria said. "Probably not."

"*Probably* not," the mayor repeated. "So then, do you think it's *probable* that a certain young girl—"

"No," Daria said. "I told you I wasn't in here."

"I cannot stand insubordination of any kind, young lady," the mayor said. "I will not abide lying. And I absolutely will not tolerate someone sneaking around behind my back, going into my counting room without my permission."

All the many times Daria had been falsely accused and falsely punished flooded back to her. "I haven't been sneaking around," Daria said fiercely. "I've been telling you the truth. What *I* cannot stand is being accused of something I didn't do."

"Well, then," Mr. Hoytie said, "perhaps the time has come for us to part company." He paused and looked down at her from his superior height. He squinted. He stroked his long black beard. "I'm going up to bed now, for I am tired after spending another long and arduous day as mayor of Hoytie-by-the . . . uh, Felicity-by-the-Lake. When I come down for breakfast in the morning, I expect you to be gone. Take your things and get out. I shall not see you again."

The injustice of it brought hot tears to Daria's eyes. To be thrown out in the middle of the night by this wicked and cruel man! The tears splashed down her cheeks, and Mr. Hoytie watched them fall with what seemed grim satisfaction. He stooped and blew out the oil lamp. Then he strode out of the room. As he passed by, Daria thought for a moment that he might actually strike her.

But he did not, and Daria, stunned, stood in the darkness listening to him whistle as he mounted the stairs and entered his bedroom on the second floor. It was then that she saw the draperies move, and out from behind them came the cat with fur the color of burning leaves and fur the color of smoke. In his mouth was a piece of paper.

Suddenly Daria heard a screech from the second floor. "You did *what*?" Mrs. Hoytie yelled.

"You threw Daria out? Without asking me? Who will work at the shop, you stupid, stupid man? Who will cook and serve us dinner?"

"Calm down, my overwrought cherries jubilee," Mr. Hoytie answered. His voice was loud, commanding, and peevish. "I'll take care of it. There are many extra children in the village."

"But she's so . . . so well *trained*," Mrs. Hoytie whined.

The injustice of the situation made Daria think she might faint. She took a deep breath as the cat sidled up beside her and dropped the paper. She picked it up and squinted, trying to make out the letters. But it was too dark. She shook her head, folded the paper, and slipped it into her pocket. "Come with me," she whispered.

Mr. and Mrs. Hoytie were still arguing as Daria and the cat paused on the second-floor landing, then quickly mounted the stairs to the attic. When Daria flung open the door of her room, she was hit by a familiar blast of hot air which had accumulated during the day. The room was tiny, but there was a window, which Daria rushed to crank open. She found she was still able to smile, as she watched the cat jump up onto the sill to survey the night.

Daria sat on the bed. "Well," she said wearily,

"I never thought this night would end with me loosed upon the wild world." She looked at the cat, who looked back at her, his eyes wide. "I know it was you who moved the ledger," she said. "But believe me, it's all right. I'm not angry."

She whipped the pillowcase off the pillow and stuffed her few clothes into it. "I won't be sorry to see the last of this place," she muttered. Then she remembered the book she'd been reading, the one she'd borrowed from Anne Wilford. She tucked it under her arm, grabbed the pillowcase, and slipped down the stairs. The cat stayed close beside her all the way.

CHAPTER

The Fateful Night Continues

No sooner had Sam delivered Caleb Withers back to his house than he heard a suspicious noise coming from around the corner. He rose up on tiptoes and hurried off to do his duty. As he made his way down Harmony Lane, he saw something sprint across his field of vision—something gray, if he wasn't mistaken—running from a purple spirea to a maple tree. Sam froze, and a shot of pure panic tingled down each of his meaty legs and arms. A wolf!

Sam stood totally still, watching and waiting. He counted his heartbeats as they thumped in his chest—to five and then to ten and then back to one again (for ten was as high as he could count). He had gotten to seven when the gray thing moved again. The hair on the back of his neck bristled. Whatever the thing was, it was carrying something white in its mouth, and this time it ran from the maple tree to the large rock that was the pride and joy of Mr. and Mrs. Spoongag's front yard. It was smaller than Sam thought a wolf would be, but bigger than a rat or chipmunk. He was flooded with relief. A raccoon? But raccoons weren't gray. Sam wasn't sure, but he thought it might be a cat.

Though few animals had been out after dark—their owners for the most part kept them locked up tight—Sam had caught a cat once before, and several dogs. He enjoyed going to the homes of their owners and banging on the doors; he enjoyed the looks of shock and dismay that crossed the owners' faces. And he especially enjoyed sweeping the owners off their feet and carrying them to the counting room.

Sam tiptoed quietly toward the Spoongags' boulder. But before he got there, the cat took off again, this time streaking to a large rock garden planted with petunias. Sam looked beyond the rock garden and guessed that next the cat would make for the stand of lilacs on the Kelloggs' large lawn. With amazing speed and in total silence, Sam tiptoed his way over to the lilacs and waited.

He had gotten rather good at this stalking. He stood tall and noiseless, and he was very pleased when the gray cat suddenly shot from the rock garden to the lilacs and hunched practically on top of Sam's oversized boots. Sam didn't move. He knew the cat wouldn't dart off again too quickly, and he wanted to relish the moment. He saw the cat inch forward and peer out into the darkness to find its next destination; he saw the cat suddenly notice the large leather tongue of Sam's left boot; and as the cat's gaze began its slow ascent up Sam's leg, Sam reached down and smoothly grabbed the cat by the scruff of the neck. But the cat was too quick. He let the white thing—a sheet of paper—fall from his teeth and used them to bite the ham-sized hand descending toward him. Sam yowled and pulled back; he kicked out at the cat but missed, and the force of his kick threw him backward, entangling him in the lilac's branches. By the time he'd regained his footing, the cat had vanished.

Shocked, Sam inspected his wound; there were two small punctures in the fleshy web by his thumb and two in his palm. Blood welled from

each of them. He put his hand in his mouth and, with his other hand, picked up the sheet of paper the cat had dropped.

There were letters on the sheet, faint and scratchy. For a moment, in his frustration, he considered crumpling up the paper and stomping it underfoot; but a faint perfume wafted toward him and he thought better of throwing the item away. He took a deep sniff and stuffed it in his pocket.

As Daria closed the door of the Hoyties' house behind her for the very last time and stepped out into the street, she felt a sense of freedom wash over her. No more working in that shop! No more serving dinner! No more cleaning house, and listening to Mrs. Hoytie prattle on, and having to write down her profound and poetical thoughts!

She'd barely gotten to the end of Orchard Street when she laughed, and knelt down, and stroked the cat who crouched beside her. "I don't know where we'll sleep tonight," she said, "but I don't care. It's warm, and the air's sweet, and . . . you must be my lucky charm. If it weren't for you, I'd still be living in that prison."

The cat calmly turned his pale amber eyes up at her and almost seemed to smile. He raised his back against her hand, then twitched his ears and darted out ahead of her about ten feet.

"What?" Daria said. She stood.

The cat looked back at her over his shoulder and began to move forward.

"You want me to follow?" Daria asked. "Lead on!"

Together she and the cat walked quickly down Lake Street. As before, the houses Daria passed were shuttered and silent. The night fell upon her and the village like a slick coat of black lacquer, sealing up every crack and crevice.

Lake Street ended squarely, and Daria followed the cat onto the footpath. *Well,* she thought, *since I'm breaking the first proclamation, I might as well break the second.* She was as familiar as anyone with the paths around the lake, and besides, the cat seemed to know where he was going.

Daria turned to stare in the direction from which they'd come. The trail had twisted among high weeds that now concealed any glimpse of the village. All she could see behind her was the faint glow in the sky cast by Felicity-by-the-Lake's three-globed streetlamps.

She thought of proclamations three and four.

"The mayor's a vain and brutal man," she said aloud, "and I belong to no one but myself." The

darkness didn't answer, and Daria set off as resolutely as she could to catch up with the cat, who
was strolling casually away from the village in the
direction of the lake.

Daria spent the night on a bed of soft pine needles and dried leaves by the lake's shore, her back
curled up against a fallen tree. The world lay so
still that, right before she drifted into sleep, she
thought she could hear the scratch of a single star
as it quavered and fell, engraving its path on the
water.

But Ulwazzer did not fall asleep so easily. He
crouched on a stump at the water's edge. From
time to time his tail flicked, but otherwise he
seemed in a trance. He burned in the cool night
air, letting off a glow as sure and as concentrated
as heated metal.

He was thinking of what had happened at the
mayor's. Though Ulwazzer knew there were no
wolves in the mountains, he'd discovered that
the mayor's son believed there were, believed
that those wolves might well come down to
Felicity-by-the-Lake in the glimmering dark. So
Sam was frightened of wolves, was he? Ulwazzer
started to devise a plan.

And after his plan was more or less complete,

he found he was still thinking about what had happened earlier—about how this girl had taken him home with her; about how he'd gotten her into trouble; about how she had accepted her dismissal so bravely, and without blaming him, and seemed even glad of it; about how she had followed him, without question, to this spot.

Somehow he'd recognized Daria the first time he'd set eyes on her, the morning he returned from his travels, when she and the mayor's wife and son had come down to the lake; somehow she was *familiar,* and he had known then that his fate was twined with hers. She had not been frightened of him, had thought him unusual rather than odd. She had given him cream and bread. And though there were many others in town who had done the same thing, none had brought him inside to eat. They had placed the bowls outside their doors.

Of all those who had fed him, the kindest had been the printer and his wife; they had a daughter, Anne. He would make sure that he took Daria there in the morning. Besides, she had a piece of paper that he thought the printer might be interested in seeing.

CHAPTER

14

A Borrowed Book

As the sun's rays filtered over the palisades of
the jagged mountains, long before they cascaded
down the wooded slopes to illuminate the lake
and warm the day, Daria awakened. It was chilly
for June, and she shivered as she knelt at the water's edge to wash her face. When she sat back on
her heels, she saw that the cat was awake as well,
lapping at the lake's gentle wavelets.

The cat seemed anxious to return to town, and
as Daria had the night before, she followed him
up the path they had taken; still following him,
she threaded the dawn-quiet streets of Felicity-

by-the-Lake. Though she had walked this way a hundred times or more, this morning everything looked different to her, as though it had been rinsed free of grime. She had changed in the night, and she saw the world through her own eyes, eyes that no longer belonged to the Hoyties.

When the cat stopped by the front door of the printer's house, Daria couldn't have been more astonished. The cat looked up at her genially and pushed against her leg. She raised her fist as if to knock, and when the cat nodded, she rapped three times. Then she hesitated, for she knew that poor Mr. Wilford had been awakened the night before by Sam, and he was probably very sleepy. But it was Mrs. Wilford who answered the door, in her nightgown and mobcap, and her eyes held a mixture of surprise and worry.

"Why, Daria!" she said. "Whatever is the matter, dear?" A look of dismay suddenly crossed her face. "That man didn't send *you* here with another proclamation?"

"Oh, no," Daria said. "Not at all." Then she remembered the book Anne had lent her. She fumbled in her pillowcase and pulled it out. "I just . . . well, I came to return this."

"But the sun is barely up," Mrs. Wilford said.

"And it isn't even Sunday. There's something you're not telling me. Come in, come in."

Daria hesitated. "May he come in, too?" she asked, gesturing at her feet.

For the first time Mrs. Wilford noticed the cat who seemed to smile up at her. "Look who it is!" she said. "Ulwazzer! Lyman used to feed him all the time, but we haven't seen him in months. Yes, of course, bring him in."

The three of them made their way to the kitchen, where Mrs. Wilford settled Daria at the table and poured her a cup of tea. Daria was sitting quite happily, Ulwazzer purring on her lap, when Anne burst in.

"Daria, look who you have!" she said. She knelt beside Daria's chair and scratched the tawny spot between the cat's ears. "Where'd you meet up with *him*?"

"I had to go out and . . . well, never mind," Daria said. "He followed me home."

"Not to the mayor's house!" Mrs. Wilford cried out. (Everyone in town knew about Mrs. Hoytie's allergies, since the woman had made such a fuss about them.) "Did you get in trouble?"

"They never saw the cat," Daria said, "but Mr. Hoytie accused me of something I didn't do and when I wouldn't admit to it, he threw me out."

"Threw you out?" Mrs. Wilford said with disgust. "Into the street? Wherever did you sleep last night? Now don't you worry, dear. I'm sure he'll calm down soon and welcome you back."

"Why would she *want* to go back?" Anne asked. "She can live here with us."

Daria blushed and suddenly wondered if Mrs. Wilford thought that was why she had come. "No, no," she said. "I really just came by to return the book—"

"Why, Daria, look who's on your lap!" Lyman Wilford exclaimed. He stood in the doorway already dressed in his work pants and leather printer's apron. He was so tall that the crown of his head almost grazed the top of the door.

"Lyman," said Mrs. Wilford, "you come right in and sit down. You won't believe this." And as all the Wilfords turned their attention to Daria, she began her story again, this time making sure to include every detail.

"Why in the world would he think you were in his counting room?" Lyman Wilford asked.

"His ledger got moved," Daria said.

"Well," said Mr. Wilford with a gleam in his eyes, "that settles that. We can't have someone living at the mayor's house who *didn't* move his ledger. You'll have to come live here where there are no ledgers not to move. I'm certain I can find lots of ways to get your hands as dirty as mine and Anne's. And our friend in your lap will have to stay as well."

Daria didn't know what to say to these good people. She was so used to feeling unwanted, so used to meanness and suspicion, to orders and recriminations and aspersions, that gratitude overwhelmed her and all she could do was smile and nod.

Ulwazzer stood on Daria's leg and arched his back. His eyes were closed, but he looked as happy as a cat who has long wanted a home of his own would look.

Mr. Wilford stood and clapped his hands together. "Now, what would you like for breakfast? Eggs? Pancakes? Cinnamon toast? Oatmeal? Grape juice? Strawberry preserves? Yogurt and honey?"

Daria realized both that she was very hungry and that no one had fixed a meal for her since her mother and father had died.

"Oh," she said. She could feel tears flooding her eyes. "That's so kind of you. Whatever you're having, thank you very much."

"But we're having all of it!" said Mr. Wilford. And he began to fix their breakfast.

15

Mr. and Mrs. Hoytie Take a Stroll

By nine in the morning, everyone in the village had taken a look at the new posters, which were inscribed

Proclamation the Fourth
From this day forward, anything
which does not belong to you belongs
to Prucilla and Jeremiah Hoytie.

The whole village was abuzz with talk. Some made fun of the mayor's vain overreaching, while others were prone to take his arrogant greediness seriously; people bitterly shook their heads as they argued with one another while hanging up their just-washed clothes, or walking to and from their places of employment, or working in their gardens. The news about Caleb Withers was also bandied about; it seemed that Caleb's mother had been so upset at the treatment her son had received that she'd suffered a severe case of nervous flibbertigibbets and had had to take to her bed.

"Are they going to snatch the cottage we live in?" asked Winona Fendrake, who had five small children. "We don't own this cottage, you know."

"It's all right, Winona," her neighbors assured her. "Fred Bunsey does, and as long as he continues to own it and rent it to you, you have nothing to worry about."

"What about the fountain in the square and the statue of Mayor Stern?" asked Rosemarie Fisher.

"They belong to all of us," Bartholomew Rivers told her.

"Ha!" said Old Man Twombley. "I wouldn't be too sure."

"And the moon?" asked Gundred Firth. "And the mountains and the meadows and the wildflowers and the birds?"

"Don't be absurd," her neighbors told her.

At ten-thirty, Prucilla and Jeremiah Hoytie proceeded to stroll the streets of Felicity-by-the-Lake. They had already solved their domestic-help problem. They had gone to the chimney sweep's, where an orphan boy worked as an apprentice and, because he belonged to no one, they claimed him and bade him run along to their house to scrub all the floors before they returned.

Now that this was taken care of, they turned their attention to the morning's special task: finding *Anything which does not belong to you.* Mr. Hoytie wore his special long-tailed, double-breasted, extra-large suit coat with the brass buttons, and Mrs. Hoytie wore a profusely flowered sun hat and carried a silk parasol. They strolled arm in arm, pointing at things—Mrs. Watney's potted geraniums; George Henry's sawhorses—and remarking how nice it would be if they didn't belong to Mrs. Watney or George Henry. Of course, Mrs. Hoytie was remembering the lake and the clouds and the swans and the bluebells. But at the moment she was in the mood for something more homespun. When she saw the plaster flamingo in Gilbert Grey's front yard, she decided she wanted it. She was not shy about telling her husband.

"And what would you do with that flamingo, my dear?" Jeremiah Hoytie asked. It stood on one leg and had a piercing green eye and was a bright pink so shocking that the mayor found himself slightly afraid of it.

"Why, you silly thing!" Mrs. Hoytie said. "I'd put it in front of the *house*, of course. Don't you think it's time we got some animals?"

"Perhaps, perhaps," Mr. Hoytie said. "But this particular one clearly belongs to someone."

"How do you know?"

"It's in Gilbert Grey's front yard, as you see perfectly well. We'll just have to buy you one." Privately he shuddered at this possibility.

"No!" said Mrs. Hoytie petulantly. "I want *that* one. And I want you to march up to the door right now and inquire if it belongs to anyone."

Mr. Hoytie looked carefully at his wife. Though he loved her dearly, he could see that her overly developed acquisitive side might actually cause him some personal difficulties. He did not like knocking on people's doors and asking them questions; he much preferred interrogating them in the privacy of his own counting room, where they hung upside down from his son's large hands. Nevertheless, he could see that if he did not do as Mrs. Hoytie asked, and quickly, she would have a falling-down fit on the street and embarrass him. So he nodded as pleasantly as he could and made his way to Gilbert Grey's front door.

He knocked four times, loudly, and then stood waiting. When there was no response, he knocked again. Evidently Mr. Grey was not at home. Relieved, the mayor turned to his wife and showed his empty palms to the sky.

"Wonderful!" Mrs. Hoytie said. "Then we can just take it!"

"Take the flamingo?" Mr. Hoytie asked uncertainly. This he did not relish in the least, since clearly Prucilla meant not that *we* could take it but that *he* could, and he did not wish to pick up the ugly pink thing and carry it through the town.

"But it doesn't belong to us!" he blustered.

Mrs. Hoytie put her hands on her hips; her face grew red and her shoulders began to shake. Mr. Hoytie feared that in another moment, she'd be lying in the street kicking and wailing and beating her fists. He hurried to her side and put a hand on her arm.

"My dear," he said in a lowered voice. "We'll send Sam around for it later, if you must have it. But at the moment, let us please continue with our walk."

Mrs. Hoytie looked much aggrieved to be leaving empty-handed, despite the consolation of getting the flamingo later. So when a red ball came rolling down the street, hotly pursued by two young boys, Mr. Hoytie said, "Look, a ball! Would you like *it*, my dear?"

"Usually I have no use for balls," said Mrs. Hoytie, sniffing. "But under the circumstances, I'd be delighted."

Her husband picked up the ball and handed it to her just as the two boys skidded to a halt in front of them. "Thanks," said one of the boys. "That's ours."

"Oh, reeeeally?" said the mayor. "And what makes you think so? As far as I could see, this was just a lone little ball, rolling down the street of its own accord."

"We were chasing it," the other boy said. "We were playing."

"That may be so," Mrs. Hoytie said. "But how do we know this ball belongs to *you*?"

"My mom gave it to me," one of the boys said.

Meanwhile Mr. Hoytie was turning the ball over and over in his hands. "I don't see a name here anywhere," he said. "As you may know, I am the mayor of Felicity-by-the-Lake, and I have just issued a proclamation which states quite clearly that anything which does not belong to you belongs to me."

"And me," Mrs. Hoytie piped.

"And since there's no name on this ball, I think it belongs to me."

"And me."

One of the boys kicked Mr. Hoytie in the shin quite hard with his pointed boot, which caused the mayor to howl and drop the ball and hop around in the lane on one foot. The other grabbed the ball and the two boys ran off as fast as their legs could carry them.

"In the future," Mrs. Hoytie called after them, "put your *name* on it, why don't you, or you won't get off so easily." Because of the flamingo, she was secretly pleased to see her husband punished. "Right, my dear?"

Her husband stopped hopping long enough to smile sourly at her.

CHAPTER

16

The Mayor's Scribblings

Breakfast had long been over, and Daria was as full as she had ever been. She'd had a little of everything, and she hoped she hadn't appeared either too hungry or too greedy. When Mrs. Wilford went off to run errands and Mr. Wilford retired to the print shop, Daria helped Anne wash the dishes, and between the two of them the work went swiftly; they talked and laughed, and Daria could feel in her bones how different it was to do chores out of gratitude, because she wanted to help, rather than because she was being forced to and was no better than a slave.

All the time the girls worked, Ulwazzer sat and watched them. And when they went up to Anne's room, he followed, and sat peacefully as they talked about the book that Daria had brought back. They both had liked it very much; it was an adventure story about a girl who ran away from home, joined the circus, and became best friends with a lion, and sometimes the girl stuck her head in the lion's mouth, and sometimes she opened *her* mouth as wide as she could and covered the lion's nose. It had a happy ending, as did all the books the two girls liked best.

They were sitting contentedly on the edge of Anne's bed when Ulwazzer jumped up next to Daria and began to paw at her pocket. Daria picked him up and placed him on her lap, figuring that he wanted to be petted. But he wrestled free, as he had the night before, and jumped back to the floor, making Anne and Daria laugh. Then he jumped right back up onto the bed and began once more to push at Daria's pocket with his paw.

"What's he doing?" Anne asked.

"I have no idea," Daria said. "It's not as though I even *know* him very well yet, but he's never done anything like this before."

"Maybe he wants something in your pocket. Do you have food in there?"

"No," Daria said. She reached into her pocket and was surprised to find the piece of paper she'd put there the night before. "Do you think this is what he's after?"

Ulwazzer began to purr loudly, and Daria even thought he nodded.

She unfolded the paper and spread it on her lap, ironing out the creases with the palm of her hand. "Why, this is the mayor's handwriting!" Daria exclaimed. "I'd recognize his scribblings anywhere." Anne craned her neck, and the two of them read the mayor's notes in silence.

When they had finished, they stared at each other in disbelief.

"Hoytie-by-the-Lake?" Anne said. "Getting rid of the cats? Of all the stuck-up, stupid—"

"But what about laying claim to people's children!" Daria yelled.

"Let's take this to my dad," Anne said. "He'll know what to do."

And so the three of them marched down to Mr. Wilford's print shop and burst in. He was bent over a tray of movable type, very intent on his work.

"You won't believe . . . ," Anne yelled.

"Wait till you read . . . ," Daria yelled.

Mr. Wilford whirled around. "Wait a minute,

wait a minute," he said, waving his hands in the air. "Not both of you at once! What's wrong?"

"Look what Daria brought from the mayor's house," Anne said.

"We only just read it," Daria said.

"It's some new proclamations and—"

"Hush!" Mr. Wilford said sternly. "Let me see." Daria and Anne stopped talking and stood quietly while Mr. Wilford read. Ulwazzer sat at their feet, his eyes on the printer's face.

Mr. Wilford's eyebrows rose and fell, and he got redder and redder. "Why of all the . . . That low-down . . . This is unbelievable!" he yelled. "No more! We won't take any more. The people of this village must finally come to their senses!"

"But what can we do?" Daria and Anne asked.

"We've got to call a town meeting," the printer said, sitting down and staring at the paper before him. "So I'll print something up, I guess. But no more posters. If those get put up, everyone will think the mayor's responsible. How about a handbill?"

"That's a great idea!" Daria said. "Anne and I could take it around and deliver it to people's doors."

"Excellent!" Mr. Wilford said. "Let's wait for

Betsy to get home. She's the wordsmith; I just put the letters together."

"What do you think will happen?" Anne asked.

"I'm not sure," her father said. "But this time it just might be good for us, instead of good for the mayor."

Congregation of Fowl

By midafternoon, all the waterfowl who lived on the lake had gathered for a confabulation. Near the reeds and rushes, close to shore, were ducks and geese and swans and loons and cranes and herons and egrets and bank swallows. As always, before they talked of anything else, they spoke of the terror in which they lived, never knowing from one day to the next if their lives would be shattered by the roar of Sam Hoytie's guns. Each of them had lost a family member or a friend; no one was untouched. For every bird the murdering blockhead had recovered, to take home for food, another ten had fallen to the surface of the lake, where their feathers had become waterlogged, pulling them under. A great heaviness now weighed upon those who remained; fewer and fewer of them even wanted to fly.

But after a while, after they had named the birds who'd recently been killed, after they'd mourned and raged, they began to argue over what exactly the newest proclamation meant.

"Surely he doesn't mean that he owns *us*," said a swan, "any more than he owns the villagers themselves."

"No more, no lesssss," the water snake hissed, but no one heard him, for he was hidden within the marsh grass.

"What I think," said a loon, "is that he'll lay claim to everything he can get his hands on, beginning with those things that no one else in the village wants."

"And what would those be?" asked a crane mockingly. She stood on one leg and looked down her long beak at the loon.

"Well, the paving stones in the street, for example. And the weeds by the side of the road."

"Certainly," said the crane. "Surely he'd want those most attractive weeds."

"Enough talk," said a snowy egret. "Rather

than arguing over what these Hoyties think they own, we ought to be figuring out what to do."

"But there's not a great deal we *can* do," the loon said. "It's the villagers who have to put a stop to this, and if they merely sigh and say this man will only be mayor for a few more months, then we're in serious trouble. If he stays true to his character, who knows what proclamations he might yet post? He could even proclaim himself mayor for life!"

This caused a great deal of burbling, honking, and general perturbation among the assemblage.

"She's right," a blue heron said. "This Hoytie seems to think he owns things which everyone knows *no one* can own. How can a single person claim to possess the streets after dark? How can a single person possess this lake? I expect that before too many days go by he'll try to take even more away from us and the villagers."

"What will we dooooo?" asked an owl.

"Ssssssomething tells me you may sssssssoon find out," hissed the snake. His sudden appearance inspired a great flapping of wings. He had twisted into view but lay on the bank at a safe distance from the water, mindful of the sharp beaks of the larger birds. "Look," he said. "Look who comessssss."

The birds all swiveled their heads in time to see a rippling of the tall weeds along the path to Felicity-by-the-Lake. As they watched, there came, in single file, the cat known as Ulwazzer, followed by three dogs—a black-and-tan coonhound, a bloodhound, and a basset hound.

The sudden appearance of these creatures was surprising, and though the birds knew Ulwazzer, they were wary of dogs. A thrill of fear rustled their feathers, and a few birds cried in alarm. But Ulwazzer held up a paw for quiet, and the birds soon settled down.

"Good afternoon," he said to the assemblage. "I've brought my friends for a demonstration."

"Whatever can you mean?" a swan asked.

Ulwazzer turned to an owl. "Let's begin with you," he said. "Would you be so kind as to call for us?"

The owl looked suspiciously from cat to dogs and back again. "Why me?" he asked. "And who are *they*?" He gestured toward the hounds.

"They," said Ulwazzer, "may hold the solution to our common problem. Now, if you please, a few melodious hoots. Draw them out for us; make them as ghostly as you can."

The owl felt flattered by all the attention. He puffed up his breast feathers and his cheeks.

"Whooooooooo," he said. "Whoooooooooooooooo whoooooooooooooo . . ."

And then Ulwazzer turned to the mourning doves. They were hesitant at first but soon joined in.

"Woooo," said the mourning doves. "Woooo woooooo."

"Not bad," said Ulwazzer. "I think we can get the job done, but you'll need to practice. And I do mean all of you. Let my friends illustrate the proper intonation." He turned to the three dogs and nodded; all three raised their noses to the sky.

And howled.

Wolves in the Mountains

That night, as Sam stepped out the door to patrol the streets of Felicity-by-the-Lake, he thought he heard, far in the distance, a high sustained cry that seemed to come across icy distances, a din filled with fear and blood and pain. It was a noise both furred and toothed, a piercing moan, a drawn-out-upon-the-wind murmur of longing and warning. It made the hair stand up on the back of Sam's neck. He gulped.

Sure, he had listened to his father tell him that there really weren't any wolves. But Sam, not his father, had been the one who'd spent all those nights walking the streets, and if the truth were told, every now and then he could have sworn . . . There had been eyes in the darkness, from time to time, hadn't there? Eyes watching him?

Because his hands were shaking, Sam stuffed them deep into his pockets, and in so doing he rediscovered the piece of paper he'd jammed there the night before. An excuse! He turned, opened the door of his house, and went back inside.

His parents were at the dinner table about to dip their spoons into a hearty fish soup. The main course—as Sam knew, for he had been the one who'd shot the key ingredient—was spitted pigeons stuffed with chestnuts and raisins. As Sam appeared at the door of the dining room, his father looked up at him and lowered his spoon. "Yes, Sam?" he said impatiently. The terrified orphan boy who had lived and worked at the chimney sweep's stood trembling in the doorway.

"I . . . I forgot to give this to you," Sam said, holding out the piece of paper.

"What is it?" the mayor asked.

"Well, I caught this cat last night," Sam said, "and it bit me and I dropped it and it dropped this—"

"Sammy," said his mother, "whatever are you talking about?"

Sam took a deep breath and started over. "I found this piece of paper and—"

"Give it to me," the mayor said, reaching out a hand. Sam offered the paper, and his father quickly snatched it away. He put it on the table and looked at Sam pointedly. "Thank you," he said. "Now you may go."

"Uhh . . . ," said Sam.

"I'm about to become annoyed, Sam," said Mr. Hoytie.

"Sorry, Dad," Sam said. "But I thought I heard wolves."

"Wolves?" said Mrs. Hoytie.

"Yeah," said Sam.

Mr. Hoytie laughed menacingly and pointed a finger at his son. "Don't be ridiculous. How many times do I have to tell you there *aren't any wolves* around here?"

"But I heard—"

"Listen, Sam," Mr. Hoytie said. "I'll tell you one more time. I made up the wolves and the snapping turtles so that the villagers would believe I had a reason for issuing the proclamations."

"So the villagers think there are wolves and snapping turtles?" Sam asked.

"Of course," his father said. "That's why they

stay indoors at night and keep away from the lake."

"Well, if *they* think there are wolves and snapping turtles, why can't I?" Sam asked.

"Because I made them up!" his father yelled.

"But I heard—"

"It was your imagination, Sam," said Mrs. Hoytie. "Though if the truth be told, I never thought you had much of one." She sneezed. She'd been sneezing all day long; it was almost as though there'd been an *animal* in the house.

"It's the wind in the trees," said Mr. Hoytie.

"The sighing of the breeze," said Mrs. Hoytie.

The mayor's eyes lit up. "The end of a wheeze," he said.

"The curdling of cheese," Mrs. Hoytie said.

"Nope," said Sam. "It's wolves."

"Now, Sam," said Mrs. Hoytie, "I'm about to get very cross with you."

"Sorry, Ma," Sam said. "Maybe . . . maybe . . ."

"That's right," said Mrs. Hoytie. "Now get on about your business."

Sam nodded and backed out of the room. He let himself out the front door and stood silently for a minute. Breezes and wheezes and cheeses and treeses passed through his mind, and he tried to make himself understand that the far-off howl he thought he had heard, the thin shiver of noise that had risen on the evening wind and then had fallen away again, was something other than wolves. And he almost succeeded. At any rate, when he began his chanting, he could hear nothing other than his own voice, and he was off.

The Hoyties had finished their soup and the boy had cleared the table and brought out the platter of spitted pigeons before Mr. Hoytie again looked at the piece of paper Sam had given him. He was in a foul mood already because it reminded him of that *other* piece of paper, the one that had been on his desk blotter and was now missing. He had searched high and low and hadn't been able to find it, but at least he had remembered all his ideas and had been able to make a fresh list.

The writing on the paper before him was difficult to decipher, and he dragged one of the candelabra over so that he could see more clearly. He was forced to read slowly, and thus each sentence struck him with special weight.

"What is it, dear?" Mrs. Hoytie asked.

"An anonymous note," he answered.

"Oh, really?" said Mrs. Hoytie. "How quaint."

She wasn't the least bit interested. She sneezed and speared a pigeon, brought it to her plate, and without further ado sliced the frail carcass down the middle.

"There's a cat, it seems," said Mr. Hoytie, musing. "According to this, he looks quite peculiar."

The orphan boy stood uncertainly in the doorway. His mouth opened as if to speak, and he raised an involuntary hand toward the table. Mr. Hoytie jumped on this sudden movement and turned to him. "You know something about this cat?" he asked. "Speak up!"

"No—No, sir," the boy said. "I . . . I just wondered if . . . Are there really no wolves or snapping turtles?"

"For *you*," Mr. Hoytie said, "there *are* wolves and snapping turtles. But for me and my wife and son, there aren't. Do you understand?"

"No—No, sir," the boy stammered.

"You'll understand when we want you to," Mr. Hoytie said. "Now, keep still." He turned back to his wife. "It says that this cat walks abroad at night and goes quite frequently to the lake. I'm shocked Sam has never caught him, because against all expectations our little Sammy has turned out to be quite good at what he does."

"I'm shocked as well," said Mrs. Hoytie. She sneezed.

"We must do something about this cat, my jalapeño cornbread."

"And what would that be?" Mrs. Hoytie asked, after blowing her nose.

Mr. Hoytie shook his head. "I don't know."

"Well, who does he belong to?" asked Mrs. Hoytie. "Surely that's a place to start."

"And you've put your finger right on the trouble, my popover. It seems this cat belongs to no one. He just comes and goes as he pleases."

"How does he *sustain* himself?" Mrs. Hoytie asked. This was a question of major concern to her and her son and her husband.

"I would guess he forages. Mice and voles and the like."

Mrs. Hoytie shuddered and felt her gorge rise. "Please, my love," she said. "Not when I'm eating."

"Perhaps from time to time someone puts out food for him."

"But who?"

"Everyone and no one, I suppose," the mayor said.

"Surely not everyone," Mrs. Hoytie said. "Are people that generous?"

Mr. Hoytie stared at the candles burning before him, and the glimmer of an idea appeared in the dark recesses of his brain. It seemed just inside the bounds of possibility that this cat had been fed, at one time or another, by most of the inhabitants of Felicity-by-the-Lake, and thus he could make a case that the cat belonged to everyone. And since it was common knowledge that the people who owned an animal were responsible for paying the fine when any infraction of the proclamations was noted . . .

A broad smile wreathed his lips. "Then I can fine everyone in the village!" he cried triumphantly.

Mrs. Hoytie stared at her husband. "Whatever are you talking about?" she asked.

Mr. Hoytie explained himself, taking his wife step by step from feeding to ownership to responsibility. Meanwhile she munched on pigeon and nodded more and more approvingly. "That is an utterly brilliant plan, my love," she said. "You've outdone yourself. So you'll have Sam bring all the villagers here, upside down, one at a time, for interrogation?"

"Yes indeed," said Mr. Hoytie. "They could all use a pleasant shaking up."

"Well, that sounds like a lot of work," Mrs. Hoytie said. "You'd better get a good night's sleep before you start anything. Tomorrow will be time enough."

As she lifted a crystal goblet to her mouth, she thought she heard, far in the distance, a strange moan falling away to a plaintive whisper. A shiver ran through her; had it suddenly gotten cold in the dining room?

"Why, that is so odd," she said. "I thought I just heard . . . no, no, no. It couldn't be. I'm sure it was nothing. Nothing at all."

"As usual, you are correct, my scrumptious Yorkshire pudding." And Jeremiah Hoytie picked up a pigeon in his two fat hands and bit right into it.

A Valiant Warning

Daria lay in the spare bedroom at the Wilfords' that night, Ulwazzer curled beside her. She was filled with a mixture of happiness and apprehension. The relief she felt at no longer being personally under the thumb of the Hoyties was immeasurable, but the *town* was still under their thumb, and she was worried about how it would all work out. Earlier that afternoon, she and Anne, together with Mr. and Mrs. Wilford, had sat at the Wilfords' kitchen table and composed the particulars of the handbill. Then Anne and Daria and Mr. Wilford had worked until dinner, and then again after it, setting type and printing hundreds of copies.

Though Daria had been eager to begin distributing the flyer, Mr. and Mrs. Wilford reminded her about the first proclamation. Who knew what might happen to her if Sam were to return her upside down to the house of the mayor? And besides, Daria thought, if the handbill was to work, it would have to be delivered at a time when people would be receptive to it. Summoned by an unexpected knock on the door after dark, the villagers might be frightened, and would possibly not even answer.

Ulwazzer had disappeared for most of the afternoon, but he'd returned at dinnertime. Now it was almost midnight and the moon was long since up. Most of the town lay swaddled in sleep, and Daria decided she ought to close her eyes and stop worrying. She would certainly need her stamina tomorrow. A cool breeze filtered in through the open window, and Daria nestled deeper under the covers, her arm around Ulwazzer. As she fell asleep, he was purring.

Ulwazzer waited until Daria's breathing was slow and regular, and then he carefully slipped free of her arm. Though he more or less considered it a waste of time, he had one more task to accomplish: he had to warn his brother and sister about the mayor's intention to ban cats. Gigamaree and Flumadiddle had not been kind to him, true enough; nevertheless, he thought he ought to act better than they, and he felt an obligation to them since they were his siblings.

He jumped up to the sill of the open window and down onto the lawn. As he had the night before—so much had happened so quickly!—he found his way to Mayapple's disreputable yard. The same pantry window was open, and once again he whispered Gigamaree's name.

Gigamaree eventually appeared, his tail still crooked, his fur still gray and matted. "You!" he said when he saw Ulwazzer. "I thought I had done away with you!"

"And how did you think you'd accomplished that, brother?" Ulwazzer asked.

"Never mind," Gigamaree said. "What are you doing here?"

"I came to warn you," said Ulwazzer. "I won't bore you with a long tale, but I've discovered that the mayor's plans for this town go well beyond his current proclamations. He has a scheme to rid the town of all cats."

"Don't make me laugh!" Gigamaree said. "What do you expect to gain from that story?"

"It's not a story. He and his wife hate cats, as you know, and he plans to banish all of us. And if anyone keeps a cat against his orders, he'll fine the person five hundred doons."

"No one has that sort of money!" Gigamaree said. "How would they pay?"

"They couldn't, of course," Ulwazzer said. "And who knows what the mayor would do to them—or to their *cat*—if they didn't pay?"

"Perhaps he'd banish both of them!" Gigamaree exclaimed. "This is terrible. Why, he might try to banish everyone and have the town just for himself!" Then the cat's eyes narrowed suspiciously. "And how do *you* know?"

"I was in the mayor's house," Ulwazzer said. "I saw the notes for his plan right there on his desk."

"Let's just say I believe you," Gigamaree said. "I have one further question. Why would you risk your hide to warn me while that oaf Sam is about? Just last night *I* was apprehended by the—" Gigamaree stopped and took a deep breath. He could feel himself venturing into territory he wanted to avoid.

"Well, if he caught you, he didn't hold you, I surmise," Ulwazzer said. "Else old Mayapple would have been treated to an upside-down jostle. And he wasn't taken to the mayor's, I know. I was there when the mayor's son brought Caleb Withers."

"Were you?" Gigamaree asked. Ulwazzer's story was beginning to sound more and more plausible. "Then why—"

"Because you are my brother," Ulwazzer said simply, and jumped down to the ground. As he cleared the fence and began his journey to Miss Gagney's, he heard Gigamaree calling after him.

"Wait! There's something I need to tell you," Gigamaree yelled. But Ulwazzer had no time to dawdle.

Just like the night before, he stuck his head in his sister's cat door and whispered her name. And this time he had a long wait, for she was not nibbling tapioca pudding but was fast asleep on her downy bed. Her name had to filter down into her dreams before she awoke.

"You!" she said. But she was strangely glad to see him, strangely glad to know that the scheme she'd worked up with Gigamaree had not yet come to pass.

"Now, listen carefully," Ulwazzer said. "I was in the mayor's house last night, and I found a piece of paper, on his desk, which stated plainly that he plans to rid this town of cats."

"My goodness!" Flumadiddle said, she who

had personal knowledge of the Hoyties' hatred of cats. "How will he do that? Poison us? Shoot us?"

"I don't know what he intends to do other than forbidding the villagers from keeping us and fining them outrageously if they disobey."

The idea brought rage into Flumadiddle's vain and lazy heart. She instantly thought of all the kindness she'd received from Miss Gagney, all the compliments and tidbits and scratchings, and it made her very angry to think that harm might come to Miss Gagney because of her.

"That's it!" she said. "I was willing to adjust to those other proclamations, but certainly not this one!"

"Daria and the Wilfords have a plan to call a town meeting about this," Ulwazzer told her. "We ought to go too. Tomorrow, you must work as you've never worked before. You must tell every cat and dog in town, and have them go to the meeting. Ten o'clock in the evening. Town Hall."

"I thank you," Flumadiddle said. "Does Gigamaree know?"

"Yes," Ulwazzer said. "About Hoytie's plan but not about the meeting."

"He'll be ashamed," Flumadiddle said, "as I am, for all the cruelties we've showered on you, and all the tenderness we've withheld. You didn't need to warn us, and yet you have. I beg your forgiveness and promise to be a proper sister to you from this day forth."

"Agreed," said Ulwazzer, smiling. "That will please me greatly. Now I must go. Remember to tell everyone tomorrow."

"I shall," Flumadiddle said. "You may count on it."

The next morning, as Daria and the Wilfords ate breakfast, there came a knock at the front door. Mr. Wilford answered it and came back with Old Man Twombley. "Betsy!" he said. "Girls! Listen to this, you won't believe it. Tell them, Upton."

"He's really done it this time," said Mr. Twombley. And then he suddenly stopped talking and pointed to the chair next to Daria where Ulwazzer lay curled. All the blood drained from the old man's face. "That's him! There he is."

Daria stood, alarmed. "What's the matter?"

Mr. Twombley was silent. He stared blankly at Ulwazzer. When it became clear that the man would not be able to speak, Mr. Wilford told them the news. "Hoytie's decided that Ulwazzer is the town's all-time champion proclamation-breaker, and the mayor's found a way to turn this to his advantage. He's claiming that since we've all fed Ulwazzer, we're all his owners, and thus responsible for all his so-called crimes. Hoytie's sending Sam around to drag each one of us to his house, where he plans to fine us nine doons each."

"Oh, no!" said Betsy Wilford, who had not yet made an upside-down trip to the mayor's. "Everyone?"

Mr. Twombley found his breath. "Yes," he said. "Everyone. At least the adults. The mayor has a voting roster and he's going down it alphabetically."

"But this may be just what we need," Daria said. Everyone turned to look at her as though she'd lost her mind. "Anne and I can go to people's houses when they've just come back from the mayor's. Will there ever be a better time to give out handbills?"

20

Inquisition

All day long Sam worked at his father's bidding, going up one street and down another, knocking on door after door, carrying the villagers one by one by their ankles to the mayor's. To make matters easier for himself, Mr. Hoytie had Sam move his desk and an empty trunk to his front lawn, where he sat in judgment for a full ten hours. It was there that Sam set the villagers down, somewhat too forcefully, and watched with his father as they got up, dusted off, and tried to compose themselves. But the mayor wouldn't wait before slamming his hand on the top of his desk. He would lean forward accusingly, spreading his fingers over the pages of his leather-bound ledger. "Have you ever," he would ask, "ever, *ever* fed a strange and foreign cat with . . . um, let's see"—his eyes would fall to the anonymous note next to his ledger—"with fur the color of burning leaves and fur the color of smoke?"

"Why, uh . . . why, yes," they would all admit, for everyone had. "But what of it?" the bravest would ask. "You haven't issued a new proclamation forbidding us from feeding cats now, have you?"

"One's pets are one's responsibility," would be the mayor's stern reply. "And I do not appreciate your sarcasm."

"But that cat is not my pet," each villager would argue. "That cat belongs to no one."

"Feeding implies ownership, and ownership, as you know, is nine tenths of the law." The mayor would pause to allow this tidbit of jurisprudence to sink in before he continued his interrogation. "Did you know that this cat feels free to walk abroad at night?" The villagers would shake their heads. "That he comes and goes frequently to the lake?"

"No," they'd reply. "I didn't—"

"*Silence!*" the mayor would yell. "No disagreeing with the mayor! That will be nine doons," he'd say, writing furiously in his ledger. "Payable

immediately. Constable, take him away!" And Sam would do as he was told.

All day long the mayor sat as his son stomped up and down the village streets. All day long the mayor asked the same questions, levied the same fines, and watched with satisfaction as his trunk filled with doons.

At one point in the middle of the afternoon, as Sam stood holding Gundred Firth by the ankles, a look of fear crossed his face. "Did you hear that?" he said.

"Hear what?" Mr. Hoytie asked.

"That moan," Sam said. "Like . . . like . . ."

"Don't say it, Sammy," Mr. Hoytie warned.

"Did *you* hear it?" Sam asked Gundred Firth.

"Hear what?" the poor woman said in a strangled voice; she'd never imagined it would be so hard to talk while upside down.

"That . . . that *howl*," Sam said.

"I heard nothing at all," said Gundred Firth, "with the blood pounding in my ears."

"I did," Sam said. His voice was resolute.

"Now, Sammy," Mr. Hoytie said ominously.

"You're both out of your minds," said Gundred Firth. And the mayor fined her nine round doons.

* * *

As soon as the villagers were returned to the places from which they'd been snatched, Daria and Anne would appear and stuff handbills into their hands. "Read this!" they'd say. "It's urgent."

"But I can hardly see," would be the answer. "The world's just spinning and spinning! My head hurts, and my ankles are throbbing!"

"Yes, we know," Anne and Daria would say soothingly. "But make sure you read this."

And as soon as the people had recovered, they would do as the girls had asked, and this is what they would read:

PEOPLE OF FELICITY-BY-THE-LAKE!

The time has come for us to stand together.
If we do not stop the Hoyties,
we will all be ground beneath their heels.
They are not content with flowerpots and flamingos.
Now they want our children!

EMERGENCY MEETING TONIGHT
10 PM TOWN HALL

IGNORE THE FIRST PROCLAMATION!

PROTECT YOUR FAMILY AND COMMUNITY!

<u>BE THERE</u>

CHAPTER

21

Call to the Hunt

It was getting dark as the mayor marked the last fine in his ledger. He got to his feet, quite pleased with the day's work. Stooping before the over-flowing trunk, he picked up handfuls of doons, letting them run through his fingers while he waited for Sam to return and carry the trunk inside to the treasure room.

"Yoo-hoo, my dear," sang Mrs. Hoytie, sticking her head out the door. "Dinner is almost ready." She smiled angelically at her now much richer husband. "I saw a chicken in the yard next door, and when I called out, 'Whose chicken is that?'

no one answered. So I yelled, 'It's mine,' and I sent the orphan over to wring its neck. He's stuffed it with sausage and chestnut and sprinkled it with thyme and rosemary and it's finishing roasting as we speak."

"That sounds divine, my nest of spun sugar," said Mr. Hoytie. "I was getting quite fed up with waterfowl. But first you must come here and see what we now have."

He held out a hand to his wife and she leapt toward him. And for a long moment the two of them stood, entranced, their arms around each other, as they contemplated the trunk full of doons.

Not much later, the orphan boy stood in the dining room doorway, waiting to serve the special dinner that Mrs. Hoytie had ordered be prepared in celebration of their unexpected windfall. The Hoyties—including Sam, who had been excused from his nightly prowl after his very hard day—sat before a table glittering with silver and china and gold-rimmed crystal. The rich aroma of roasted chicken filled the air.

"Let us bow our heads and give thanks," said Mrs. Hoytie.

The heads of Sam and the mayor snapped forward, and Mrs. Hoytie delicately cleared her throat and began.

"I'm thankful that I'm so smart and beautiful," she said, "and blessed with a talent for profundity. And I'm thankful that I'm married to a rich man who is richer every day and who will give me everything I need and much more that I *don't* need . . ." Here she hesitated, and a slight blush rose to her already rouged cheeks. "Though today I'm just a bit annoyed at him." She cleared her throat again and her voice soared. "And we're both thankful for our son, who's strong enough to pick people up by their ankles. Not every family has such a son."

Sam grinned at the unaccustomed praise, though he kept his eyes closed.

"Well said, my little crème caramel," said Mr. Hoytie, raising his head. "But why in the world would you be annoyed at me?"

"I'm pleased, of course, with all the doons you collected," Mrs. Hoytie said. "But you so used up Sam's time today that I couldn't get out on the lake, and who knows what profound inspirations have been lost forever?"

"I don't want to go to the lake anymore," Sam said.

The mayor harrumphed once. "I *am* sorry to

have taken up Sam's time," he said—though he wasn't, particularly. "But tomorrow, I'm afraid, you'll again have to do without him."

"Tomorrow as well?" Mrs. Hoytie said. "I can't stand it! And why don't you want to go to the lake, Sammy?"

"Snapping turtles," Sam said.

"I have plans for him," the mayor said. "I've decided to advertise a hunt."

"What snapping turtles?" Mrs. Hoytie said. "You know there aren't any snapping turtles."

"I thought I saw one. Or two," Sam said.

"May I have some attention?" Mr. Hoytie yelled. "I said I was planning a *hunt!*"

"Oh, boy!" said Sam, who loved hunts of any kind. "What sort of hunt? A treasure hunt? An egg hunt?"

"A cat hunt," the mayor said.

"A *cat* hunt?" said Mrs. Hoytie. "What do you mean, a cat hunt?"

"Well," began Mayor Hoytie after clearing his throat a few times, "here's my idea. It does no good, no good at all, to have this cat with the strange fur stalking the streets of the village. The people of Felicity-by-the-Lake may have been fined, but that cat is still on the loose. And now that he's cost the villagers nine doons apiece, I'll have them help me find him. Tomorrow I'm posting an *Order of the Mayor.*" Jeremiah sat back and laced his fingers on his great round belly. "First, I'll install Sammy here in a booth by the central fountain—"

"You mean I can't be part of the hunt?" Sam asked.

Mr. Hoytie sat forward and slammed the table with the flat of his palm. "Confound it, son," he yelled, "business before pleasure!" He turned to his wife. "As I said, I'll install Sammy in a booth by the central fountain and I'll sell cat hunting licenses. Everyone who wants to enter the cat hunt will have to pay ten doons for a license. And I'll advertise a reward of five hundred doons for this cat." He smiled. "Dead or alive."

"That makes no sense to me," said Mrs. Hoytie. "Why would you pay such a large sum of money?"

"It's basic economics, my succulent peach. I've impoverished most of the villagers, so they'll do anything for money. Surely they'll be willing to gamble ten doons on the possibility of making five hundred. There are three hundred and fourteen adults of voting age in the village, and a conservative estimate suggests that about half of those will purchase licenses. That means I stand to take in fifteen hundred doons, and will only have to pay out five hundred when that cat with fur the color of burning leaves is finally brought to justice. And that, my little macaroon, means we will be one thousand doons richer!"

"Well!" said Prucilla Hoytie. "That *is* a good idea."

22

No Time like the Present

By five minutes before ten o'clock that evening, the town hall was packed. Caleb Withers was there with his mother; Felix Mayapple was there (with Gigamaree skulking behind him). Mr. and Mrs. Lionel Penrose were there, as were Mrs. Watney, whose geraniums Prucilla Hoytie had coveted, and Gilbert Grey, whose flamingo had been taken by Sam. Even Miss Edna Gagney, Jeremiah Hoytie's employee, was there—not to mention Flumadiddle. In fact, every man, woman, and child, every cat and dog in Felicity-by-the-Lake had stuffed themselves into the town meeting room. There was a tumult of sound. The men and women held cudgels and tin pans and rakes, and they were angry and impatient. They kept looking at the clock, waiting for the exact moment when the big hand would hit the twelve and the meeting would begin.

Daria was beside herself with excitement. She couldn't believe how well their plan had worked, and how solidly the townspeople stood, determined to rid themselves of the scourge of Hoytie. She sat near the back of the room, with Ulwazzer crouched on her lap. He was trying to stay as small and unnoticeable as possible, but that hadn't prevented his brother and sister from finding him and coming over to say hello. Both of them were as friendly as cats could be, and Ulwazzer saw that even Gigamaree was sorry for his nastiness and was trying to make a fresh start.

Daria bent over and stroked them both. "Hi, Flumadiddle," she said. "Hi, Gigamaree. How do you know Ulwazzer?" But of course they didn't tell her.

When the clock struck ten, the crowd fell suddenly silent, and from the front row of seats, Lyman Wilford stood and turned to face the villagers.

"Thank you all for coming," he said. "It's good

to see so many friends and neighbors." He paused. "Outside. After dark."

There were whoops and hollers, wild applause and great laughter. Someone yelled out, "Wilford for mayor!" and soon the crowd began chanting it until the name *Wilford* echoed in the recesses of the room, scaring the bats from the belfry.

Mr. Wilford held up his hands for silence. "No, no, now, wait a minute," he said when he had their attention. "I wanted to be mayor last January because I thought I had good ideas. But now I realize that every mayor tries to push his ideas on everyone else, gently or forcefully. And this current mayor of ours—"

He was interrupted by a chorus of catcalls and boos, barks, and howls. People stood and raised their rakes into the air.

"I know you're very angry," Lyman Wilford said. "I'm angry too. But remember that it's not all his fault. It's our fault too. We let him get away with all this nonsense."

"What do you mean?" someone yelled from the back of the room. "We all went to his house and complained, didn't we?"

"But we obeyed him," Mr. Wilford said. "In spite of the fact that we know there aren't any wolves in the mountains or snapping turtles in the lake."

At first there was confusion, and then the people of Felicity-by-the-Lake began nodding.

"And why did we obey him?" Wilford continued. "Because we were afraid of Sam. We didn't want to be grabbed by the ankles and held upside down. It was easier to live with what had been forced upon us than to change it. We thought January would come soon enough.

"Daria," he called. "Bring Ulwazzer up here."

At the perimeter of the room, Daria stood, Ulwazzer in her arms. The crowd parted and she passed among the townspeople to stand at Mr. Wilford's side.

"You all know this cat," Wilford said. "We each got fined today because of him. But because of him we also know what the mayor has planned for our children and our future. And it might be a good idea if, from now on, we followed Ulwazzer's example. He lets no one cage him; he follows no unjust laws."

"But what about Jeremiah Hoytie?" Lionel Penrose yelled.

"String him up!" cried Felix Mayapple.

"Let me at him," Caleb Withers snarled.

The crowd erupted, but Lyman Wilford held up his hands once more and the townspeople quieted. "We'll figure out how to deal with Hoytie," Mr. Wilford said. "But first, can we agree that from this moment on he is no longer our mayor, his word means nothing, and his proclamations are null?"

"Hurrah!" the townspeople shouted.

Mr. and Mrs. Hoytie lay in their warm bed, trying to sleep. Mrs. Hoytie had washed her face with lemon juice and yogurt and now lay humming to herself with two cucumber slices resting lightly on her eyelids. Next to her, her husband was wide awake, restless, thrumming his fingers on the coverlet and running over the details of his cat hunt in his head. He could just imagine the line of villagers handing over ten doons for hunting licenses. He could just imagine the tumult as the villagers, carrying cudgels and tin pans and rakes, thrashed through the town and the surrounding land. He could picture the victor, returning to the central fountain with the errant cat held upside down by its hind legs. So vivid were the scenes in his head that he couldn't get to sleep and finally he threw back the covers, slapped the edge of the mattress, and declared, "Prucilla, as I've always said, *there's no time like the present!*"

"You've never said that before in your life," Mrs. Hoytie answered. She would have sat up and glared but she didn't want to disturb the cucumber slices.

"Why, indeed I have, my little raspberry mousse. And now I'm off to Lyman Wilford's to have him print up my mayor's order and the hunting licenses."

"But surely that can wait until—"

"I mean not to put off until tomorrow what I can do tonight. Half the secret of success is surprise, my dear—and you remember how successful we were with the posting of the last proclamation."

"But why not send Sammy?"

"Yes," said Mr. Hoytie, pausing. "I could do that." He settled back onto the pillow and stared at the ceiling. But the more he thought about it, the more difficult it sounded; he'd have to rouse Sam, who took forever to wake up, and then take him downstairs to the counting room, and then draft the mayor's order for the cat hunt and make up a rough copy of the license he had in his mind, and . . . All things considered, it sounded more difficult than simply taking the reins into his own hands.

"No, my dear," he said, sitting up again. "I believe we should let the boy sleep. He really did yeoman's duty today; can you imagine holding over three hundred people upside down? Besides, it's been ever so long since I took a moonlit stroll and thought my profound and poetical thoughts. So don't even try to argue me out of it."

"Well, if you must," Mrs. Hoytie said. She felt a slow burn settling in: she'd been denied Sam's rowing talents for two days running, and now her husband was about to leave their bed in the middle of the night to go out into the dark and have profound thoughts. "Don't wake me up when you come in," she sniffed.

"There's no need to be huffy," said Jeremiah.

But Prucilla obviously thought there was. "And be sure to lock the door after you," she said. Then she readjusted the cucumber slices and pretended to be asleep.

Mr. Hoytie splashed some water on his face, donned his blue waistcoat with the brass buttons, and briskly walked downstairs and out into the evening air.

It was a splendid night. The moon had recently risen, round and textured as a hammered gold plate. Stars punched through the sky's black fabric like silver studs, glittering so fiercely they seemed about to burst into flame. But even in the midst of such beauty, Mr. Hoytie could not shake the thought of his wife's ill temper. She was a difficult woman, moody and prone to irritation. She'd quite spoiled his pleasant and optimistic frame of mind. And since he did believe firmly in business before pleasure, he directed his steps toward Wilford's place. Better to get his mayor's order and cat hunting licenses printed first. As soon as he'd talked to Wilford, he could concentrate on his moonlit stroll. Perhaps he'd feel better then.

The CLOSED sign on Lyman Wilford's door did not deter the mayor. He pounded with his fist three times, heavily and with portent. There was no answer. He pounded again. Looked at his watch. It was almost eleven o'clock, but even if Wilford was already asleep, how long could it take to get up and come to the door? Could it be that the man wasn't home? Sammy wasn't patrolling tonight, after all, and perhaps Wilford was taking advantage.

"Wilford!" Mr. Hoytie yelled. "Lyman Wilford!" He banged until his fist was black and blue, but around him the village lay as quiet as if no one lived there at all. Mr. Hoytie grunted, then turned to leave, thinking as he walked of ways to punish the insolent man. He laced his hands behind his back and stuck out his great watermelon belly so that the brass buttons on his blue waistcoat bristled all the more. Ah, well: there would be time enough tomorrow to consider a punishment. At the moment, he still had profound thoughts to think.

CHAPTER

Sleeplessness

In her bed, alone, Mrs. Hoytie tossed and turned. Her teeth itched and the bottoms of her feet felt cold. Her husband was not yet back, and she was filled with wrath. It was just like Jeremiah—so selfish! thinking only of himself!—to walk out into the night like that, without even asking her if she wanted to accompany him. She wouldn't have, of course, but she'd have liked to be invited. And the way he was monopolizing Sam's time! Two whole days, one after the other, without his services as boatman and rifleman. Who knew what sorts of brilliant rhymes would be lost again tomorrow? And who knew what they'd have for dinner?

She turned over once more, the cucumber slices fell from her eyes, and she realized that she wouldn't be getting to sleep anytime soon. Although she wasn't normally so afflicted, she occasionally had trouble sleeping, and she thought of the various remedies available to her. She might have had a glass of warm milk with honey if Daria had been there to make it for her, but Daria wasn't, and the orphan they'd brought home just wasn't working out. She might have taken a hot bath with lavender oils if she hadn't already bathed twice today, putting her skin in danger of turning prunish.

Perhaps what she needed was some conversation. But then it occurred to her that with Daria and her husband gone, there was only Sam to talk to, and he—she had to face it—was not a particularly adept conversationalist. Nevertheless, she sat up, put her feet into her fluffy bedroom slippers, wrapped a robe around her shoulders, and shuffled off in search of her son.

She stood outside his door and listened to his snoring: great heaving rips in the night's quiet. She knocked quite loudly and called his name, but the snores continued. So she pushed open the door and stepped inside. Sam lay in his specially made bed—specially long and specially wide and specially supported by timbers underneath—on his side with the covers thrown off, revealing his rather hairy, exceptionally large bare feet.

Mrs. Hoytie bent over him and shook his arm, and with a vast rumble, Sam rose slowly from the depths of unconsciousness. He rubbed his eyes and snorted, he arched his back and stretched his legs. The room—indeed, the whole house—shook. Finally settling down, he looked wildly around him until his eyes fastened on his mother.

"Ma?" he said. "Is that you? What's the matter?"

"Nothing, Sam," his mother said. "I was just . . . just a bit lonely, I guess."

"Where's Dad?"

"Oh, he went out some time ago, to get some things printed for that cat hunt of his. You know your father, he has very little patience. He just couldn't wait until tomorrow."

"He should have sent me," said Sam.

"Yes, I know. That's what *I* thought," Mrs. Hoytie said. "But your father wanted to let you sleep. Silly man."

"So what do you want to do?" Sam asked. "Play canasta?"

Sam was horrible at all card games that required thinking, so Mrs. Hoytie changed the subject quickly. "I was wondering," she said, "about going to the lake, if you want to know. It's a lovely night—the moon is almost full. And as he's told you, your father plans to utilize you all day tomorrow. Since he's out walking, thinking profound thoughts, perhaps I should take a moonlight float and see what occurs to *me*."

"You want to go to the lake . . . tonight?" Sam asked.

"Yes," said Mrs. Hoytie. "I believe I do."

"But *I* don't want to," Sam said. "What about the wolves and snapping turtles?"

"There aren't any wolves and snapping turtles!" his mother yelled.

And so it was that Mrs. Hoytie went to her room to dress, and Sam pulled on a shirt and pair of pants, and the two of them left the house on their way to the lake.

They hadn't gone far when Mrs. Hoytie thought she heard a high wild croon, which filled her with mournfulness and the sharp edge of fear.

"What's that noise?" she asked.

"See?" Sam said. "I told you."

"Don't be silly, Sam. Can't you get this into your head? Your father made them up. But whatever that noise is, I don't like it, and tomorrow I will have your father issue a proclamation against it."

Moonlit Swim

The rowboat sat where Sam had left it the last time they'd been to the lake, and the pile of pillows was still inside. Mrs. Hoytie looked forward to lolling as long as she liked, with Sam at the oars, while she dangled a finger in the water and thought profound and poetical thoughts. It would surely soothe her, as it always did, to be reminded of her own superiority to the majority of human beings, who could no more rhyme than fly.

On the shore the water was hushed, and the waves that lapped at Sam's and Mrs. Hoytie's feet could not be called waves at all, or even wavelets.

They were more like the breathing of the lake, the small rise and fall of its great dark chest. And far out, the round disc of the moon floated, breaking into pieces whenever the breeze picked up. Around it the water was pocked with glittery moonscales.

Mrs. Hoytie sighed in satisfaction. "This is just right," she said. "Now let's get to it, Sam."

Sam grunted and pushed the rowboat, with his mother safely lounging inside, into the water. He jumped in, and the boat rocked madly, then settled as he began to pull on the oars. In no time they'd reached the middle of the lake where Mrs. Hoytie had seen the golden pieces flash, and she was disappointed to find, as she hoisted herself up and peered over at the dark water, that the moon had floated elsewhere. She lay back for a moment and let the evening wind waft over her.

"It's pretty, isn't it, Sam?" she asked.

"Yeah, Ma," Sam said. But he didn't seem convinced; his eyes darted nervously here and there.

"Pretty witty ditty," she said brightly. "Shall we play the rhyming game again?"

"Uh . . . OK," Sam said, a bit hesitantly.

"Just give me a word then, any word," Mrs. Hoytie said.

As before, all words flew from Sam's big head.

He stared out at the lake, so still and dark, until he thought, with a stab of fear, that he saw, bobbing on the surface, what looked like a snapping . . .

"Turtle!" he cried.

Mrs. Hoytie's eyes narrowed, and she put her hands on her ample waist. "Will you not desist, Sam?" she said. "How many times do I have to tell you?"

"I saw one, Ma, I did," Sam insisted.

"So what if you did?" Mrs. Hoytie said. "Turtle. Hurtle, girdle, myrtle."

And then she thought she heard that *noise* again, the one she wanted her husband to issue a proclamation against. It rose on the wind and hung high, sustained and plaintive, before falling. Over the lake, sharing the sky with the moon, a few clouds had gathered, like mattress stuffing torn in angry shreds. The noise put her teeth on edge and brought dark thoughts. She remembered the clouds she'd seen the last time she'd been at the lake: marshmallow fluff, puffy and cheerful. She felt far from cheerful now. What was she doing in a rowboat, on a black lake in the middle of the night?

As Prucilla stared out over the water, the lake didn't seem such a friendly place. The mountains she wished to own—and the untold wealth beneath them—looked dark and forbidding. They had certainly been standing there a long time; in fact they were probably older than she was. But after all, what difference did that make? And the stars seemed bright and cold and everlasting; the sky, like the lake, was black, very black, imperially black, a great, dark page on which the clouds were inscrutable writing. She stamped her foot, but the feeling did not go away and the mountains did not lie down in submission.

Well, enough of these gloomy thoughts! She was Prucilla Hoytie, the wife of the mayor of Felicity-by-the-Lake—soon to be Hoytie-by-the-Lake—and she and her son were the only ones here. They owned the place. Who cared what a mountain thought? Who cared for a star's good opinion? Resolutely she sat up and looked at the moon's reflection lying placidly on the water, just out of reach. "Sammy," she said, "I want you to row over there where the moon is. I want it."

Sam looked at her doubtfully but picked up the oars. "OK, Ma," he said. He took a few strokes, but just as they were about to reach the moon, it darted off again. Mrs. Hoytie leaned out after it and urged her son on. He made quite a ruckus, sending waves here and there with his oars, and the moon broke apart and seemed to fly in different directions.

"Why, look," Mrs. Hoytie said, pointing to the shards of bright gold. "It's just like a shower of doons. Isn't that lovely?" She reached out so far that she was almost in danger of falling, and she glided her hand through the water as if to scoop up the doons.

"Look out!" Sam yelled, standing up. The boat rocked violently.

"Look out for what?" Mrs. Hoytie said petulantly. "I almost had it."

"A turtle?" Sam asked.

"No, you idiot. The *moon*."

"Did you see one?" Sam asked.

"A turtle?"

"Yes."

"When?"

"Now."

"No, did you?"

"I think so."

"Where?"

"There." Sam pointed to a spot about twenty feet from the boat, and Mrs. Hoytie squinted, trying to see better. She leaned forward over the edge.

In Sam's imagination the surface of the lake began to ripple, and for a moment he saw hard

humped shells and sharp claws and leathery
necks and heads with small mean eyes. He could
feel the panic rising in him like a tide, and he
staggered around in a circle, waving his arms.

The boat rocked so wildly that Mrs. Hoytie lost
her balance, and though she flailed her arms in
the air like backward windmills, she couldn't pre-
vent herself from plunging into the lake. She was
suddenly chilled straight through, and when she
came up for air, she had algae in her mouth.
"Help!" she cried. She yelled as only Mrs. Hoytie
could yell. She beat the water to a froth with her
hands. "Sam!" she screamed. "Sam! Help me!"

"Coming, Ma," he said. He tried to reach her
hands with an oar, but by now he was beyond
any manner of sensible thought and he too lost
his balance, capsizing the rowboat and throwing
himself into the lake along with his mother
among the broken shards of moon.

Mrs. Hoytie, as you know, was strong as a water buffalo, though she tried to hide it, and when
she saw that her son would not be rescuing her
anytime soon, she began to swim toward shore.
But Sam, fired by his absolute terror of snapping
turtles, was already well ahead of her and beat
her by a mile.

CHAPTER 25

A Run for His Money

Jeremiah Hoytie walked down one deserted street and up another. Occasionally he tripped over a paving stone that had jostled itself loose since he'd become mayor. Well, that would need fixing: he couldn't be stubbing his toe whenever he took a stroll. He noticed a number of streetlamps with broken globes. Who was responsible for keeping the village in good repair? Surely that wasn't the job of the mayor. But this was a profound thought he'd have to consider later. Right now he was too taken by the awareness of how totally his proclamations had succeeded: he had the whole town to himself.

Without really heeding where he was going, he found himself on Main Street, headed for the central square. The fountain splashed sedately, and the bronze statue of Mayor Stern, the first mayor of Felicity-by-the-Lake, seemed unruffled and serene. Mr. Hoytie crossed his arms on his chest and considered the statue. As cast, Mayor Stern was an attractive man, tall and distinguished. He wore a top hat and morning coat, and he stood holding a cane that rested on the ground at his feet.

Mr. Hoytie had never considered it before, but it suddenly seemed the proper time to have this statue taken down and replaced with a statue of himself. He pondered for a moment how he ought to look. Would it be a good idea, he wondered, to make himself—in his statue version—less stout? Perhaps the statue version should be clean-shaven. And what should he be wearing? A military uniform, perhaps? Perhaps he ought to be seated upon a horse.

With great effort he clambered up the hewn granite blocks on which the statue stood. Mr. Stern was considerably taller than he, and quite cold to the touch. Nevertheless, Mr. Hoytie kept his balance by throwing a companionable arm around the back of the earlier mayor, and with him, he gazed out over the town to the dark mountains in the distance.

From this vantage point he saw in the moonlight the high weeds that grew at that place where the lake path began. He watched in amazement as the weeds parted and two hulking figures burst into view. One of them had a voice of some sort, though the voice sounded more like that of a banshee than a human being. It was really quite frightening. "Halt!" yelled Jeremiah Hoytie as the figures approached. "I am the mayor of Felicity-by-the-Lake, and I command you to stop where you are."

"And I am your wife, you great big nincompoop!" screamed the banshee. Now that they were nearer to him, Mr. Hoytie could see that one of them was indeed his wife, and the other his son. They were both dripping wet.

"Why, Prucilla!" he said, rather shocked. "Whatever are you doing?" But she and Sam had stopped, and now Sam was trying to speak, and raising a big ham-hand to point in the opposite direction, toward the town hall.

Mr. Hoytie turned completely around just as a mob broke into the street, quickly moving toward him and his wife and son.

Clumsily Mr. Hoytie climbed down from his position next to Mr. Stern. The villagers were bearing down on him with steadily gathering speed, screaming his name, brandishing cudgels and tin pans and rakes. *What are they all doing outside after dark?* he wondered, his breath high and tight in his throat.

But he had no more time to wonder, for in a great surge they were upon him, surrounding him and Prucilla and Sam. For once his wife was speechless.

"Hoyties!" screamed the villagers.

"Good evening," Jeremiah Hoytie said, trying to make his voice as round and deep and authoritative as possible. "What can I do for you, good citizens?"

This seemed to incite an even greater frenzy in the people closest to him. Gundred Firth ran forward and pulled his ear. He looked at her in alarm. For a moment he thought that perhaps he had never left his warm bed, had never gone to call on Mr. Wilford, but instead had fallen into a deep slumber and was now experiencing a nightmare, brought on perhaps by an allergic reaction to chestnuts. And this feeling intensified as the crowd parted and Daria appeared, carrying a creature he had heard about but never seen, materializing as if from his imagination.

It was a cat, and its eyes were pale and cold, and its fur looked as if it were on fire. And suddenly Jeremiah Hoytie knew he was awake, because following Daria came a man he knew too well, a man he'd gone to call on earlier and who had not been home.

"Jeremiah Hoytie, you scoundrel," Lyman Wilford said. "Let me issue a proclamation! By order of the entire village of Felicity-by-the-Lake, you are no longer our mayor."

Of all the things Mr. Hoytie had expected to hear, this was not among them. He suddenly felt deeply aggrieved at his neighbors' ingratitude, and he pulled himself up to his tallest height. "Mr. Wilford," he said sternly, "I won that election fair and square, and there's no need for your bitter feelings. And *that*, by the way, is the cat who cost each of you nine doons. I would think his life would be in danger."

"It's not *his* life that's in danger!" the villagers yelled.

Mr. Hoytie stood uncertainly. He brushed at his clothes and tried to look kindly at Lyman Wilford. "Now, Lyman," the mayor said. "May I call you Lyman? Why don't we repair to my house for a bit to drink and eat, and we can talk this whole misunderstanding over."

"No, I don't think so," Lyman Wilford said. "The whole town will want to be in on this conversation. In the meantime, we'd like our money back. As we know, every doon you've stolen from us is recorded in that ledger on your desk."

Jeremiah Hoytie was planning all sorts of concessions, if need be, but this demand took him utterly by surprise. "No!" he cried. "No, no, no! I will leave this village if I must, but I'm taking that money with me. It's my money; I earned it and it's mine."

The more he stared at the snarling townspeople, the more their noses elongated and their eyes gleamed savagely. He was breathing heavily now, in dismay, snorting; his vision was blurred. Then Mr. Hoytie did something that no one would have expected of someone so watermelon-bellied and generally slow. Fired by fear and greed, he vaulted over the nearest townspeople and pummeled his way through the rest, and began to run as fast as he could toward Orchard Street and his immense stone house. All at once the villagers were after him, and in his addled state, with the blood pounding in his ears and his eyes hot and stinging, they seemed, as they fell silent and merely chased him, like nothing so much as a . . . a rush of *wolves*, gray scrawny wolves, their eyes flashing and their claws clicking on the paving stones. In his imagination their large crimson tongues lolled in their mouths and their sharp fangs gleamed in the moonlight.

Mr. Hoytie's feet pounded and he looked about wildly, anxious to avoid a loose stone that might trip him up. He was unexpectedly nimble, and he jumped from here to there, inspired by terror. He had never run so fast in his life, nor had he needed to. But Jeremiah Hoytie had made a career of escaping from tight places, and he saw no reason why Felicity-by-the-Lake shouldn't be one of them.

He could feel his heart heaving in his chest as he darted down Evergreen Lane and made a swift turn into an alley that served as a shortcut to Market Street. Behind him he could hear the thrumming of the wolves' paws and the harsh rhythm of their panting. He took a huge breath and one of his bristling brass buttons popped loose and sprung into the air as though shot from a gun. Then another let go, and pretty soon they were popping as frequently and loudly as popcorn. His garters loosened on his calves and he could feel them slipping down; without the garters to hold them, his silk socks puddled at his ankles.

His hair was a mess, flopping this way and that on his forehead, which was beet red and streaming with sweat. His beard felt cumbersome, itchy and strange, and he resolved to shave it when he got a moment. His silk shirt came loose and its long tails flapped in the wind, revealing from time to time his pale and bouncing belly. He looked, all things considered, quite disreputable. But now was not the time to worry about appearances. If the pursuing mob caught him before he got home, the result would be neither profound nor poetical.

Faster he ran, and faster. He made the turn from Market Street to Orchard Street, and now it was clear sailing to the outskirts of town and his house. But then, ahead of him on the street, he saw something shiny, and round, and made of gold. A doon, a single doon, lay in the street where someone had dropped it. A single doon, as lovely a thing as there was in the world to Jeremiah Hoytie, and though he knew it wasn't in his very best long-term interest to salvage it, he couldn't stop himself. As if hypnotized, he skidded to a halt and stooped and fingered it, and held it in his hand, where it felt cold and smooth and very sweet. So happy was he for that second that he failed to hear the accumulating hubbub behind him, and in the next instant the villagers were upon him, and that was that.

CHAPTER

26

Happy Ending

Jeremiah and Prucilla and Sam Hoytie were picked up by the villagers and carried through the streets, and in their wake all that remained was a single doon, lying on the street's paving stones, glinting in the moonlight. They were taken to the town jail and locked up, and the villagers decided that January would be soon enough to decide what to do with them. But now it was summer, and the villagers had wasted too much of it already.

On Hoytie's counting room desk, Lyman Wilford found the infamous leather-bound ledger,

and while he sat and crossed off name after name, the townspeople stood in line and retrieved every doon that had been illegally taken from them. But much more importantly, they got back the village's fine name as a place where people were kind and good and unafraid to speak their minds.

As for Daria, she lived happily with the Wilfords. The memory of the Hoyties slowly began to dim, and at last she felt as though she had a family again. And of course Ulwazzer lived there too, though he remained true to himself and came and went as he wished.

He visited Gigamaree and Flumadiddle almost every day, and when he didn't, they visited him. And since Gigamaree spent so much time at the Wilfords', he became a sleek and jaunty cat. His tail straightened out and he grew quite tame and even-tempered, and he finally abandoned crotchety old Mayapple to live with Flumadiddle. But Flumadiddle still received most of the spoiling and got bigger and bigger under the all-too-indulgent hand of Edna Gagney.

The rest is easy to tell. In remarkably little time, the streets of Felicity-by-the-Lake were repaired and all the broken streetlamps replaced. The ice cream shop stayed open past midnight, the cider parlor seemed never to close, and the two cafés did a booming business. Everyone seemed to want to make up for the time they'd lost by staying out longer and later than they ever had before. Window boxes and planters overflowed with petunias and geraniums and the red spires of salvia, and fresh coats of paint appeared on many houses. There were picnics and concerts and swimming races in the lake, and the waterfowl— who had sounded so much like wolves after some practice—slowly began to trust the townspeople again, though memories of Sam Hoytie never completely went away.

As autumn faded into winter and the first filaments of ice crept across the lake's surface, it seemed the entire village and all the world around it had been restored to their earlier selves. This year, with a house to go to whenever he wanted, Ulwazzer didn't feel the need to roam, and so he stayed in Felicity-by-the-Lake. He was there to celebrate New Year's Day with the villagers, who issued a joint proclamation:

No more mayors!

And they lived together peaceably with the lake and the meadows and the mountains and the waterfowl and the fishes.

As for the Hoyties . . . to say they became re-
habilitated would be to say too much. Though
many people in the village wanted to hurt them
very badly, cooler heads prevailed and the three
were merely hung upside down by their ankles
for an hour each day. On the anniversary of Mr.
Hoytie's election, he and his wife and son were
released from jail and banished forever from
Felicity-by-the-Lake. They were last seen climb-
ing the mountains, squabbling among themselves, in search of other villages whose people
they could take advantage of.

The next spring, hedges again hung heavy with
roses and the meadows were dotted with wild-
flowers—columbine and lupine and Indian paint-
brush. Birds nested in the trees, and on the lake,
ducklings and goslings followed their mothers,
and trout leapt, catching the sun on their fishy
tails.

And every night, as the sun set behind the
mountains, the people left their houses to stroll.
And as they passed Daria and Anne walking with
Ulwazzer, or Lyman and Betsy Wilford handing
out pamphlets, they reminded themselves of
what was theirs and of what could be lost in a
twinkling if they stopped thinking for themselves,
if they did merely what they were told to do, if

they stayed in their houses and closed their eyes
and shut their mouths and allowed themselves to
get used to anything at all.